IN THE SHADOW OF CROWS

"M.V. Feehan's In the Shadow of Crows is a book of immense tenderness, grace, and emotional acuity. I admire Feehan's subtle attention to states of yearning and loss, and to the secrets we reveal and conceal—from ourselves, and from each other. She deftly maps the ways we navigate our internal worlds in the face of uncertainty, anxiety, shame, fear, hope, and love. Which is to say, as she writes, 'that jumble of history we carry. The world only we know because of the steps in our wake.'" — Jared Bland, editor and former publisher, McClelland & Stewart

"Poetic in its telling—M.V. Feehan's stories weave through time with recurring characters in the varied moments of a life.These people who live in or are connected to the town of St. Anne's experience hope and disappointment, small dreams and painful realities. Throughout the narrations a Greek chorus of crows foretell the fates that await the men and women whose lives are forever changing.... From a high school crush to the tragedy of a miscarriage to family ostracization, Feehan's characters endure the burden of being alive, but they also live lives shot through with the joy of friendship, unexpected bureaucratic kindness and acts of tenderness." — Frank Macdonald, (*A Forest for Callum and Smeltdog Man*)

"A poignant view of lives passing with crows from a children's rhyme poised at the margins of each story. Feehan has a deep and sensitive understanding of human nature and a relentless focus on each individual working his and her way through the maze." — Phyllis Barber, author of *The Desert Between Us* and *The Desert Above*

"Feehan successfully evokes nostalgia but more profoundly finds poignancy in each symbolic line, which is mirrored in the precision of her writing. The result is a mosaic that is at once dreamlike and realist. The struggles and moments of joy feel epic despite her remarkable concision." — Chris Benjamin, author of *Boy with a Problem*

IN THE
SHADOW
OF CROWS

M.V. FEEHAN

Baraka
Books

MONTRÉAL

ISBN 978-1-77186-347-6 pbk; 978-1-77186-359-9 epub; 978-1-77186-360-5 pdf

Fiction Editor: Blossom Thom
Cover and Book Design by Folio infographie
Proofreading: Melissa Bull
Editing: Blossom Thom

Legal Deposit, 2nd quarter 2024
Bibliothèque et Archives nationales du Québec
Library and Archives Canada

Published by Baraka Books of Montreal

Printed and bound in Quebec

TRADE DISTRIBUTION & RETURNS
Canada – UTPdistribution.com

United States
Independent Publishers Group: IPGbook.com

We acknowledge the support from the Société de développement des entreprises culturelles (SODEC) and the Government of Quebec tax credit for book publishing administered by SODEC.

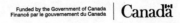

For my Theos: husband and son.

One for sorrow, two for joy
three for a message, four for a boy
five for silver, six for gold
seven for a secret never to be told

"Well," said Crow, "What's first?"
God, exhausted with Creation, snored.
"Which way?" said Crow, "Which way first?"
God's shoulder was the mountain on which Crow sat.
"Come," said Crow, "let's discuss the situation."

~ Ted Hughes

Table of Contents

One for Sorrow
Hart's Crossing: 1945

On the day he died, Emmet had been restless. As weak as he was, he couldn't stay in bed. It was August 17, 1991. Awake since dawn, he blamed the pink light that bled into his room for his state. It left him soft—emotional. His house, which he could see from the window of his room at St. Anne's hospital, beckoned. The upstairs dormers of the old colonial came and went from view depending on the sway of the alders in front of it. He knew everyone was home—telling stories at the table or on the back patio looking toward the hospital occasionally and thinking, *Poor Da.*

Poor Da indeed, he thought. Emmet rubbed his sternum and followed the incision planned for his chest wall: *sliced and sawed open and my poor heart seen and handled.* He shook the image away and eased from the bed into his slippers. He tested his balance. Confident, he grabbed the housecoat Lily brought last night and wandered into the hall. He felt the wrapper of his stash in the pocket of his robe and walked to the end of the presurgery unit to an unlit recess. Summer waved its leafy branches from every window but still, the image of his open carcass invaded his thinking. It was the boys he'd seen in war that haunted him—he knew what ribs and lungs looked like—he'd seen them from the deck of his ship in the open Atlantic drifting in and around the water after battle, torsos ripped and half-emptied. Young bodies floating as dumb as wood upon the surface—their thin faces and pale limbs unbothered by the dark ocean or anything anymore. His leg twinged. Emmet shook his head again and teetered.

At the end of his smoking nook there was a window. The view: an alley without sun and a slim vista at its end. He tucked the heel of his hands beneath the middle sash, braced and pushed it open. *Shit,* he whispered when the seal of paint cracked loudly. He listened a moment before pulling a stack chair close to the window then put a slipper on the sill to muffle a possible slam. The cork shoes of a nurse approached. Alice, a neighbour—the same that slipped him the smokes and lighter—peeked at him from the corner of the alcove, her index finger to her lips. She grabbed the cross off the dark wall.

"Hum," she said loudly as her spongy steps receded.

"It's okay, ladies," she sang to others at the nurse's station, "that crucifix fell again." Emmet settled his breathing and lit a Belvedere. The warm smoke moved through the rooms of his body like it was home. If he inhaled it slowly, it wouldn't catch on anything and start him coughing. He leaned toward the open window and blew his breath into the shadows outside. Lightheaded and happy, he noticed a crow at the edge of the alley. He turned away from it as his girls did when they were small and looked to the sky for another bird to raise the count to two: he could use two crows today.

Emmet dubbed the smoke off on the sash and saved it in his robe for later. Reaching for the slipper, his grip failed. The shoe disappeared. Stupid hand, he thought. Then his arm dropped beside him like a sausage and a numbness slipped like a snake through the arteries of his neck and shoulders. His mouth wouldn't close. He could move his eyes still but the light at the end of the alley didn't offer what he longed to see: his pretty house with the black trim and the leafy alders on the town side, the lilacs and carnations you saw only from the lane and the packed brown earth between the out-buildings in the yard where the chickens wandered. For a moment he was there, cresting the top of the lane; the kids from infant stages to older selves crowding that sacred ground. Their voices filled his head:

"Da, oh, Da—you look good … sit here," Fin patted the bench beside him.

"Lift me, Da," Annabele, at four, held her arms high, grabbing at his clothes. The others, Teresa and Carlie clawing at his robe—crying. James crawled toward him one minute then rode his bike away the next. *Too many, I can't*, he thought, *I'm done*.

"Emmet, darling." Lily burst through the sunporch door and ran toward him. *Dear Lily,* he thought, *I am leaving.* They were all in the kitchen now. The table, set. Lily was her younger self—she darted between the stove and the fridge and the dishes on the counter. Emmet was outside on the patio then, cupping his hands around his eyes to see them all through the pane. He struggled to breathe: he wheezed and landed back in the dark hall with Alice. The nurse had punched his chest. Air made it to the floor of his lungs and anchored him to the present. Pain cut across his torso. His limbs were numb now. His view—the sea beyond the narrow brick corridor outside the window. Something like fairy dust sparkled above the surface of the Gulf and for a moment he smelled the sea through the open window. Between the water's edge and himself he saw a corner of the old railway yard with the faded sign he knew read Hart's Crossing though the letters were long worn away. *That crow again*, he thought—flapping like a black rag between him and the world outside.

Frightened by the fallen slipper, the bird tore from the ground, her wings brushing the brick walls of the alley. She settled on the moulding outside the glass and cocked her head. A descendant of generations of crows along this coast, she knew the man's face on the other side of the pane. The small woods at the bottom of his land had always been the night roost for her and the flock. Her forebears had crossed paths with him through the years, and crows share what they know. Fed by generations of railway men who flung bread from the trains, these birds followed the tracks and had witnessed Emmet's return from Europe when the letters on the station's sign could still be read. Men were to be watched, she knew.

On June 29, in the last year of the war, Emmet was the only passenger disembarking the early train at St. Anne's station. He descended the steps slowly, holding onto the rail as long as possible before placing his cane on the terminus platform. Behind him, a voice announced: "Hart's Crossing, ten-minute stop." When both feet were planted beside the staff, Emmet looked for Lily.

"Are we early?" He turned to the steward who'd waited for him to descend before passing him his duffel bag. Emmet hooked the handle of his cane inside his trouser pocket to free his hands. He received the bag and eased it to the ground, steadied himself then tossed the bag on his shoulder. He waited for the answer. The steward pushed his cap up off his forehead and nodded toward the clock above the terminus entrance:

"Don't think so son—11 a.m. Can you make it okay?"

Emmet turned toward the bench along the station's wall and gave a Chaplin-like twirl of his cane. "This thing's for show," he said and waved to the older man without looking back.

"She'll be here soon enough, Romeo." The steward looked on a moment longer.

"Emmet. The name's Emmet," the soldier yelled back, irritated.

When he reached the building, he took a breath before turning and lowering himself onto the bench along the wall. He closed his eyes. The voices of workmen could be heard as they jumped from the train to begin the redirection on the roundhouse tracks. Another voice—the ticket seller—seemed close. There was talk between the ticket man and another, something about the day's transport.

Beside the window in the hospital, Alice kneeled in front of Emmet. She had a hold of both elbows and shook him gently:

"Emmet! Emmet!" She yelled his name again and again; louder each time and every time, she shook him harder. She called to the nurses down the hall for a gurney. Three of them arrived with a stretcher. The mechanical squeaks bounced off the bare walls as they lowered it. Emmet winced at the sound, his thin body twisting away from it.

Between the four nurses, they lifted the old man onto the cot.

"I'm waiting for Lily," he managed to say.

"Yes, yes, we'll get her," Alice assured him and ran ahead toward the desk.

He liked the ceiling lights passing overhead but not the nervous breathing of the nurses. Their words quivered. As they passed the desk, Alice—on the phone—told Lily to *come now*. The doctor was paged. In the room, they transferred his light body easily to the bed. The youngest of the three nurses took his wrist in her hand and looked at her watch; another grabbed a pressure cuff and slid it up his arm—his crepey skin folding like fabric beneath the strap. The third, and most senior RN among them, wound the vertical window open and pulled a rosary from her sweater pocket. She kneeled on the hard floor beside his bed and began the Apostle's Creed.

"Where's Lily?" Emmet cried whenever he had enough breath. He was no longer in the room, no longer a 77-year-old man.

He was twenty-seven, and walking the terminal platform of St. Anne's station. Home after three years of service.

The train pulled out after its ten-minute stop—the hush of its engine swallowed by the hills as it cater-pillared south. The whistles and chugging and the yelling voices of the workmen were soon replaced by birdsong and the bored sighs of the soldier's own breathing. The air was still and hot and a screen door slammed several streets away.

The terminus sat on the last road before the shore in the farming hamlet of St. Anne's. The tracks led there after running through low-treed mountains until just before the station where the trees were kept clear and the light spread freely on the slope to the sea. After the darkness of the forest, even on cloudy days, passengers shielded their eyes a little when that last turn was made.

For the traveller who ended up on the platform, there were some amenities: a fellow at the ticket booth, a clean bathroom, a cigarette and pop machine, and a large parking lot on the village side of the establishment for the family and friends of those being met.

Emmet was disappointed by the quiet. He'd been ready to laugh and talk loud amid the confusion of a large crowd. He longed to touch his wife—to feel her lips at his cheek, seek the curves of her body through the light summer dress that he knew she'd be wearing.

"You home for good, soldier?" An older couple, the only others there, had been pacing the platform and stopped in front of his bench.

"Yes sir." Emmet swallowed the pill from under his tongue.

"That's good, that's good." The man removed his hat and tapped it against the loose fabric of his dark trousers. He held the jacket of the suit with the little finger of his other hand. An expensive summer suit, Emmet thought: this guy did alright—worked behind a desk all his life by the looks of him. And she, he'd seen the likes of her before; bringing goodwill boxes to his mother's door. Replying *No thanks,* to her offer of tea: no notice of the scones on the table made for their coming, no notice of his mother—twitching, embarrassed—unsure of the protocol amid such exchanges.

"Is the leg hurt bad?" The man wiped his forehead with the collar of his suit. The woman looked on with a tight smile, her eyes in shadow behind the dark mesh that fell from her small cap.

"Na," Emmet replied. He would not call the man sir again: "I just have to be good to it for a month or so an let it heal up." The three of them were quiet, all of them looking at his leg.

"Yes—well," the man stammered, interrupting the silence: "Ellen dear, why don't you sit over here." He guided her to the next bench and she sat on the far end of it, folded her hands on her lap and leaned forward, keeping watch for the next train.

"I'll just be here then," she spoke, not looking at her husband.

The next train was due at two o'clock. Emmet guessed that Lily had gotten confused about the time, which meant he would wait through the noon sun until then. They had decided to meet here and spend the night at the Seaview Inn before driving up to his mother's place in St. Rose. It was from here he left three years ago. They'd spent the night at the Inn—awake for the most part. He, slipping into shallow naps with dreams that jerked him back to consciousness—to the warm fleshy comfort of Lily and the tears that fell sideways onto her pillow.

"Can I get you something from inside?" The man was pointing to the pop machine with one hand and feeling for his wallet with the other.

"Maybe I'll get a drink of ...." Emmet pressed his hands against the bench and pushed himself up. But the man moved toward him saying,

"No, no ... I'll get it. What do you like? Root beer?"

"A ginger ale would be nice, thanks." Emmet was left looking at the woman when her husband made his quick exit into the station. She'd been staring in his direction but looked away quickly when Emmet returned the glance. She began smoothing out the lap of her dress with quick short strokes. Her husband came back with three bottles gripped between his hands. He sat them on the bench by his wife and passed her one. She took a sip then set it beside her—already forgotten. He brought Emmet a bottle and motioned a cheer before they swallowed. "Smoke?" He offered Emmet his packet of Players Plain.

"No thanks." Emmet felt his shirt pocket for his own. A small tin of painkillers rattled inside their packet. So still was the air that he glanced at the woman to see if she'd heard. He couldn't be sure with the sun in their view but he thought they'd locked eyes for a moment—a breeze had lifted the veil from her face. Emmet turned away quickly—a little ashamed to have the pills so close—to need them so handy.

He would have popped one had he been alone. He wished that the man would leave him to his day-dreams of Lily and the swim they'd planned to take in the sea; about the lobster dinner they'd order with potato salad and beer afterward. And how the salt would taste on her back and shoulders later, skin to skin, amid the rumpled sheets of a Seaview bed. He would lay behind her then—his hand beneath her breast—his fingers at her heart, pulling her to him again and again as he cast his soul amid the waves of heaven.

"John McCormick's my name." The man squashed his cigarette into the planks and offered his open hand to Emmet.

"Emmet Carrol." Emmet shook McCormick's hand, repulsed by its softness. "Are you from here, Emmet?"

"No. I grew up in St. Rose."

"St. Rose," the man repeated the name slowly to himself. "You would have gone to school here then—in St. Anne's?"

"Ya, I spent a few years here." Emmet knew what was coming next: he'd known a Sammy McCormick on the baseball team. A tall guy, should've been athletic but wasn't. He smiled a lot and didn't appear to care if they won. He had a sort of child's nose that hadn't seemed to grow at the same rate as the rest of him had—the same nose that this Mr. McCormick had.

"You might know my boy then—did you know a Sammy McCormick?"

The man smiled—this is our connection, said the smile, we've struck common ground here. His red eyebrows lifted to the middle of his forehead and his mouth was open, waiting.

"Ahh," Emmet feigned a recollection. "No—I didn't know anybody by that name." He slapped a fly on his elbow to avoid the man's face. He hadn't wanted the conversation. Especially if he had to talk about Sammy, whom he hadn't really known. They did a science project together in grade ten; his attention to detail bothered Emmet. Girlish, he thought.

"Oh well, that was a big school wasn't it?" The man's voice was calmer now. "I mean, it serviced the whole county and there were bound to be kids you wouldn't know." He pulled his handkerchief from his breast pocket and wiped his face. "Well, Emmet, I guess you're waiting for someone, are you?"

"Ya." Emmet forced a smile in the other's direction.

"Good luck to you, son."

Emmet watched McCormick walk to the north end of the platform. He shook out his suit coat and pulled it on over his thick arms then drew the handkerchief out again and blew his nose. A crow had glided past him and landed on a gatepost beside the station— her wings flapped a little before she found balance; her head turned to the humans for a moment then scanned the pasture that the fence once bordered. *One Crow Sorrow,* Emmet remembered the rhyme from Primary. His mood had begun to sour: where the hell was Lily, he thought. You'd think after three years apart she'd get the time right. The lie he'd told McCormick bothered him; a *white lie,* his grandpa would have said—*the harmless kind that God can forgive.* He reached for the pills and glanced at Mrs. McCormick.

She was in the same stiff position, leaning forward, looking south with her eyes on the tracks. He wondered why they were there. He'd noticed them talking to the ticket master when he first got off the train. There seemed to have been confusion about passengers. He'd heard the station master apologising for the mix-up and then McCormick's loud voice:

"Okay, I see then … we'll just wait for the next one then: the two o'clock it is."

The rhythm of the train had begun to sound in the distance.

"John," Mrs. McCormick spoke out for the first time—her hands reached in the direction of her husband. John walked toward her hastily.

"Yes, yes, Ellen," he said assuredly. "I'll take care of it." He was beside her now, holding her hands in his. The face of the locomotive had just rounded Long Point. "I'll get the car and back it up to the platform." He pulled himself away from her grip: "I'll take care of it," he said again.

"I'll go with you," she began to rise but stumbled as the heel of her shoe wedged in the deck.

"Please Ellen, just wait here." Their voices grew louder, competing with the noise of the approaching train. Mrs. McCormick stepped out of the shoe.

"Okay ... okay," she was yelling now. "Go on then, get the car." She glanced blindly in Emmet's direction before kneeling to wriggle the shoe free.

Emmet felt a hand on his shoulder. He hadn't heard Lily approach. Her touch was foreign. Rousing. He moved his fingers beneath hers and lifted her hand to his cheek. She walked around him, knelt before him and pushed her face into his shoulder, mumbling something he could not make out. He closed his eyes and pressed his face into her hair, smelling lemon shampoo and soap and sweat. Her curls caught on the stubble of his chin. He was home and alive and holding Lily.

She helped him stand and stood back.

"You're better looking now," she said and pushed against him again. She reached behind him and pulled him to her, fought the urge to press his pelvis against her then settled her head sideways on his chest.

"So are you," he whispered, bending his head toward hers.

He was surprised by her smallness; surprised he'd forgotten. Her frame, beneath the dress, made him think of a sparrow. Her face, when she pulled away, was flushed and thin. Steering them toward the car, she stood aside for him to walk abreast but he pulled her to him again. Her breath was warm on his neck, then on his chin, then at his mouth. The kiss passed. The flesh of her temple and cheek pressed against his own and they held each other a moment longer.

When Emmet's eyes lifted to the world again he saw the McCormicks over Lily's shoulder. John, with the help of a steward, was sliding an oak box into the back of their family wagon.

In years to come, Emmet remembered this like a painting but never described it in words. Always, he saw McCormick's large frame beside the dropped tailgate, a steward with downturned eyes and tilted head, Sammy's coffin protruding a tad, the sun inside the car bleaching everything to obscurity while at the windshield—a crow, trapped and wild, beat her black wings against the pane. Mrs. McCormick sat in the front seat, patting her hair and touching her hat—fluttering within the car like a captive bird as they loaded her son into the back of the family Ford.

For his last breath, Emmet's face was turned to the window; his gaze upon the highest branches of the familiar alders. Lily's hands, warm and chafed, held both of his in her grip. She tucked her face between the pillow and his cheek:

"I love you I love you I love you," she whispered repeatedly in his ear. Beside them, the crow he'd watched earlier flew through his room to the inside ledge of his window. She paused on the sill for a moment before the youngest nurse chased her from the solemn event. Emmet knew she headed for shore and he envied her that. He'd read somewhere there is no place on earth without crows. *All they've witnessed*, he thought as he exhaled, *from their perch in the trees and their flying above us, and their gathering of crumbs that we toss from a lifetime; maybe, in the end, they'll take me, too.*

Two for Joy
You are Marvellous: 1985

The sign appeared like a small miracle. A white roadside panel at the foot of a steep grade: Frank'n Fra's Café.

She predicted the interior—the brick wallpaper above the cook's window, the downturned cups on pre-set tables, the plastic greenery along the sills to the highway. She draped her jacket at a table to affect her intention to stay and proceeded to the dim hallway where she knew the bathroom would be.

"Have you come far?" the waiter asked when she returned to collect her coat.

"St. Anne's," she said, then eased into a chair.

"Far to go?" he asked as he sauntered away—his wide hips swaying between the chequered tabletops. He stopped at the counter and looked back for her answer.

"Leave the woman alone, Frank," his wife teased him from the cook's window. Her assistant smiled beside her—a young boy with an after-school job who, likely, lived in one of the five homes on this corner of the road. She'd heard him tell the cook about the bullet shell he'd found on his walk there. The cook had responded with a whispered "Ooh ...." and you knew that she turned to him with great interest between their kitchen tasks.

There were other customers: locals who conversed softly and seriously in a few of the corners, and she knew that if she needed anything from their tables that they'd smile and offer it to her. She looked out the window more than she did at her book and listened to the quiet talk in the café—glad to be among them; happy that the bathroom was free when she arrived and that her cup was full when she returned to the table.

She pictured the shell the boy had found and wondered where the lead had fallen. She'd found many in the woods and on the shore as a child; drawn to the colourful plastic jacket: pained for the distant target. She could not imagine the violence of it in the quiet scene before her, although she knew the shell meant the real damage was elsewhere.

At the edge of the building, there was a phone booth. She was reminded of a movie she watched as a child that she was not supposed to be watching. Her older siblings didn't tell her to leave when it was on and so she stayed, shocked and unnoticed on the couch beside them. The girl in the film had answered a call in a booth on a quiet road like this, and came daily to that spot afterward because the voice on the phone had told her to. The girl disappeared one day, her parents crying at that spot and a policeman shaking his head. There was a warning within the tale but she was never sure of what, and she daren't bring attention to herself by asking.

The waiter took her plate away and offered dessert: "Rice pudding tonight," he said as he walked toward the kitchen. She anticipated the warm cinnamon, the milky mush, the crusty top, and ordered a bowl.

Outside, the day was fading. The woman gathered her book and bag, and pulled her jacket from the back of the chair. She would drive with the lights on not seeing much of the country she passed, but she could cry in the dark at least, even howl if she wanted; arriving at her brother's house by midnight. Already, she could hear his steps to the door, his half grumble as he unlocked it, his shrug on seeing her and saying her name in a resigned way as he stepped aside for her to enter. She could have the couch in the basement he'd said on the phone when she called from Magdalene House. And in the morning, after hardly sleeping, she would hear the sounds of his family: of he and his wife exchanging times and lists, and his children yelling and laughing and slamming doors. She would rise then, ascend to the messy kitchen to drink the last of the coffee and clear the dishes while their cat looked on indifferently.

And so, before she left the café, she looked at her book again and thought about staying longer. She touched the drawing of the Angelus on its cover and followed the delicate lines that shaped the back of the praying woman's foot: the heavy pencil that formed the Achilles. She envied the woman's wisdom. To kneel for something, to bow her head, to be studied and loved and rendered tenderly. She did not look at the people as she left the café. Her eyes were red and wet and they might ask if she were alright.

In the parking lot, backing away from the store, two crows flew from the veranda rail and knocked a small sign from the post. She was happy to see the crows, and the promise of joy from the old rhyme lifted her spirits: *One for sorrow, two for joy*.

"Grab at it," she imagined her mother saying. But as the darkness settled upon the highway, she considered her destination.

"You've burned your final bridge," her brother had said the last time she'd seen him—pulling his chair to the couch where she slept in their mother's kitchen.

"Teresa," he spit her name out like poison. She half-expected him to hit her; fling her to the floor as their father had in his fury at her inability to understand how quickly a drunken woman loses everything.

"You think only of *you*," her brother spoke slowly. His lips close enough to spray her cheek. She turned to the wall and focused on the singed lilies that floated upon the pattern. She'd helped her mother hang this paper: "Match it here dear," the thick hands of the older woman slid the paper slowly upon the wall to meet the previous strips.

Her mother hadn't guessed about her stash in the sunporch. Didn't catch on to her daughter's forays there until a stagger, a slurred sentence, and Teresa's final misstep on the lowest rung of the ladder—her backward fall and the dipping tray splatter. Her mother, silent, helped her onto the couch, then stepped outside to the first spring day of the year.

"You're already dead," she whispered as she waved her hand and shook her head. Her mother prayed outside, fell to her knees—offered everything up in exchange for her daughter's soul.

Recalling that, Teresa closed her eyes on the water lilies. But beneath her lids another image crowded her: flames from the open lid of the stove hit the ceiling. She saw her own hideous figure fumbling around it, dousing a fire that could have taken everything: And though she managed to stop it, the paper was blackened—the walls ruined.

The memory was vague, as much of her memory was: she remembered hiding bottles clearly though—the tinkling of them against each other as she squirrelled new ones beside old ones in her favourite spots. And waking sick from foggy nights, sometimes slipping out of strange beds without looking back at who she'd left there, of being ushered out and driven home, and softly mauled by whomever she passed. Hearing whispered concerns and sometimes enduring the screams of those who'd "had it." And her sore, nauseous body, its blinding headache, and the shame she pulled on everyday like clothes. The last words from her mother ran through her head like a tune she could not let go: "I pray for you, darling." The old woman: her eyes bowed at the table, her head dropped low—her praying hands clasped above it: "I pray and pray," she repeated.

Her brother, Fin, standing by the door, motioning silently for her to pick up the belongings she'd thrown in a borrowed bag and meet him at the car.

And so, they drove the three hours to rehab: he doing the only thing he knew how to do, and she enduring the verbal blows.

She was approaching her brother's exit when a line came to her from an old school text: "The gods will give you chances ...."

She imagined the little café would be closing now, and the boy would be starting his short walk home. She flicked her turn signal on and remembered the next line: "Know them." She was surprised that the poem was coming back to her. She realised that the year she'd studied that poem was the same year she worked in a café like the one she was in today, not much older than the boy. She began to slow for the exit. A rain had begun and grew heavier. The wipers pushed the water about the windshield loudly. As she listened to the wipers, their sloshing two syllabled sound became a phrase: "Don't go," said the rain and the wipers. And the more she indulged this folly, the clearer the words became. But the poem was coming back as strong: "You are marvellous ...," said the poem. Its power spoke to her directly. One evening in her high school café, she remembered reading it to the owners and they listened with interest to her reasons for liking it. In the dim light of that restaurant she was safe: sheltered by kindness. She longed for that feeling, and with that remembered the *Help Wanted* sign the crows had knocked over as she backed away from the shop. She thought of tomorrow, and of her brother and his family, and of her mother outside on that spring day—broken. She remembered the end of the poem and said it aloud to the empty car, "The gods wait to delight in you." She repeated it several times while she passed the exit and turned off her signal; then made a U-turn when the traffic permitted.

Three for a Message
Borders: 2003

Part I: The Dream

The dream, like most dreams, did not present itself as
such. There was nothing fantastic about it until the
end. It began with Annabel driving along the main
street of her hometown in late fall. She was never in St.
Anne's in autumn anymore but that was not a hitch in
the dream. The rain, in five-degree temperature, set a
damp cold in her bones but she felt happy for the heat
in her small car with the windshield wipers clearing
the drizzle from her view. The silver oaks along that
road had already lost their leaves and lined the street
like beggars—their bare arms reaching.

Annabel was a homebody and, even in the dream,
was glad to be heading to the warm rooms of her old
house where she could look upon the weather through
the melty glass of the ancient windows.

But one thing nagged at her as she made the turn at the end of town toward her childhood home. There'd been a pair outside the Country Store—a man and child stood under the awning looking distressed and cold. They were black, which was unusual as St. Anne's was a primarily white rural Nova Scotian town. Their T-shirts were thin and ripped and the child clung to his father's leg. She hoped that Al, who ran the store, would invite them in. She hoped that someone driving past would pull over and offer help.

Annabel had had a plan: though in reality she didn't eat meat, in the dream she planned to set a stew and get back to her book, to doze in the big chair while the rain tapped against the window. Or to cry all day if she wanted. She'd lost three souls in the last year and there was never enough time to grieve. Her mother's passing took the biggest bite. She loved her older sister and brother, but neither offered the unconditional love her mother had given her. That that was gone scared Annabel like nothing ever had. In the months since she'd lost the three, she'd looked for signs that they were still about— an early feather on the step or a crow's call at dusk would have been enough. But there was nothing she could hold to as proof of their presence. No sign of eternal life—no inkling that the connections nurtured on this side of the grave reconnected in spirit after our last breath.

Consequently, there were dark hours for her regarding the random aspects of birth and death: all of this knocked around inside her, even in the dream.

When she pulled into her yard—haunted by the helplessness of the two she saw on the sidewalk and knowing no one else would help—she turned the car around and headed back to town. The street was bare now, but as she turned around in the co-op parking lot, she eyed the pair under the wide overhang of the store. Pulling in, she saw that the child—a toddler—was crying and staring directly at her. The father wiped his son's face with the edge of his shirt and lifted the boy onto his hip. She leaned across the gear shift and opened the passenger door. Annabel didn't speak but once the man had settled in the seat beside her and after pulling the child onto his lap, she wiped the rain from his cheek by way of apology and took the boy's hand to her mouth and kissed it. The scent of his skin was familiar. The man nodded a thank you toward her as though the intimacy of her touch was normal. Annabel reached to the back seat for a car blanket and covered the two with the soft flannel throw.

She remembered that a thrift store had opened in the old railway station and headed toward it—they'd need clothes and boots if they were to stay. The Hart's Crossing sign had faded but the integrity of the old station held. She dropped the father and son close to the door and parked the car in the old lot behind the building. Annabel ran through the drizzle and smiled at the two who'd waited for her before entering the store. They nodded for her to go first.

She stepped into a wide storefront that contained a sea of circular racks beneath the flicker of long fluorescent bulbs. Closest to the door stood her mother—the first inkling of the fantastic in the dream. She looked just as she did when Annabel left home for the first time. Her hair in a salt and pepper bob and her slacks a little twisted where her lower belly bulged. Her mother's arms—white and thin—reached for her from a floral blouse. Annabel saw that her mother had tucked a locket beneath her collar before the embrace and as she walked into her mother's arms, saw the pendant was a small impression of the liberty statue. It pressed against their chests as the older woman pulled her tighter. She felt the warmth of her mother's skin beneath the shirt and touched the small bumps of vertebrae along the older woman's back. Her shoulder blades—*wings,* her mother called them—were flush against the muscles there as they should be in a hug. But just as Annabel was assessing her breath and heartbeat, her mother pulled away: "I know, I know ..." she said, and continued, "There's no time, dear. Take these jackets—they'll need them."

Her mother—nodding and smiling, pushed her glasses in place with a dainty grip around the frame as was her habit in life. "Pay attention," she whispered without looking up.

The soft tones in her timbre returned a longing that Annabel had not measured till then and the knowledge of her mother's death landed heavily upon their exchange. She felt her heart would burst: that a river of grief would flood the tiles beneath their feet. Falling to her knees, Annabel cried without shame for the losses everywhere, for the two she had in tow, for her brother and sister who did not have their lives anymore, for everyone on the finite journey of life. Annabel raised her eyes to the relentless glare of the store lights and keened the words: "All goodness is gone, all goodness is gone," repeating it like a mantra until she woke.

Part II: Waking

The bedroom was dark but for the Boston streetlamp outside their window. Her husband asked in a whisper if she were alright and she mumbled that she'd had a dream—that she saw her mother and her heart felt full. The numbers on the digital clock flashed 2:05 above the red light of JAN 6.

Annabel felt for her socks on the floor, pulled them on beneath the covers then slipped from the warm bed. The January wind was unusually cold and that made the bones of the old colonial rattle. She paused after every few steps to make sure her husband and son weren't disturbed by her footfalls.

At the bottom of the stairs she grabbed a sweater from a hook and continued toward the sunroom and the red file cabinet where all their documents were kept. She was hunting for a letter in a file. Land shenanigans had been stirring within weeks of her mother's death so Annabel wrote their lawyer to articulate the legacy her mother had made known while she lived. After her mother's touch in the dream—the sign she'd been waiting for—she sought reassurance that what she wrote was, as the letter stated, true to the best of her knowledge.

The radiator hissed in the living room. Annabel lifted the bottom of her nightie over it to store its heat in the fabric before entering the coldest part of the house. She stepped into the sunroom and eased open the top drawer. The *Mum* tag was the highest among the terrain of labelled folders. She pulled the manila envelope from the file noting the hard feel of one corner.

In the kitchen, Annabel emptied the contents of the envelope onto the table. Two Canadian passports toppled out followed by a two-page letter that slipped on top of the tiny books for a moment before floating to the floor. She scooped the papers from beneath the table—perplexed that the passports were stored in the *Mum* and not the *border* file.

Annabel grabbed a pillow from the rocking chair and set it on the kitchen radiator. She settled on the cushion and read. Satisfied, she returned the letter to the envelope, gave the chair back its pillow, then picked up the passports and brought them to the zip bag in the file where all their border papers were stored.

As she started up the stairs, she heard the rocker—still rolling as though something heavier than a cushion was returned to it. It was then that she saw the cards on the floor beside the table. She recognized the small white visas—the ones her husband and son needed to renew annually because they refused to be U.S. citizens. The boy thought it a game to be on the same team as daddy in this ongoing debate about citizenship in America.

"This is not my country," Annabel's husband would say. He felt hopeless about its future.

Their boy would run to his side and giggle. "Daddy and me against Mommy," he would sing, taunting her until she grabbed him squealing and laughing, until he yelled, *he-l-p m-e D-a-d-d-y* which ended in his favourite thing—a family dogpile in the middle of the floor.

So each year, they explained to American Immigration at the crossing why her son and husband did not proceed with the *privilege* of gaining citizenship. Annabel never used the term dual for her own status. No need to rankle Homeland Security in that fraught hour between countries. She presented her American passport only and answered whatever was asked of her in a soft-pedalled truth.

But a tide of alarm rose within her now as she eyed the cards on the floor. She couldn't remember the last visa renewal. They did so each year at the end of August at the Calais crossing when they returned from their summers in St. Anne's. But this year was different. She ran quickly back to the kitchen, grabbed the cards and read them beneath the light of the stove. In the circular stamp below their names the expiry date had passed by three months.

"Shit." Her body stiffened. "Shit, shit."

The cards trembled in her hands. Six times they'd crossed the border in the last year, but in the fog of grief the annual paperwork lost its importance. Their hearts were broken, which must have been apparent to the officers who asked nothing more when Annabel answered the reason for their visits. The virus had touched everyone with death and perhaps the guards had grief of their own to nurture. Even the Americans, always more on edge than the Canadian officers, would nod respectfully and wave them through.

But this lapse in renewal meant scrambling and legalese; their lives upended. Her husband and son could be deported. For all the complaining her husband did about living here, he loved his work and the team he worked with. Her boy adored his daycare teacher and the yard behind their house he called his park—wide and treed where the girls next door lavished him with attention. After so much loss she dreaded any change from the comfort he found in the steadiness and safety of his home here.

It was 3 a.m. Annabel began calling the borders where their visas could be renewed. Her first call went to the Maine crossing at Calais where they always renewed the paperwork. The officer, who conferred with another while he spoke to her, told her to get her husband and son out of the country *NOW*. Perhaps they were worried too that it was on their watch that the Canadians had slipped past. She pulled an Atlas from the bookshelf to study the border and to find new crossings. Annabel tried to simplify the story with each call. She sought pity for the bad year:

"Our losses were great—none of us were thinking."

"Anybody can tell that story, mam, you've got to get your guys out and maybe in a year you can get them back in, but there's no guarantee."

With each call, her anxiety grew. She saw their lives fall apart like a fractured puzzle—one they could never peace together again in St. Anne's—not with her history there: the drinking, the men, waking cold on roadsides then drinking more to swallow the shame. The town was too small to forget, too bored to forgive. Annabel's chest tightened, she sighed and closed her eyes on the room; that her boy should pay for her sins and struggle as an outcast on the narrow roads of that town would finish her.

She continued calling, trying to hide her fear when she spoke with immigration. Since 9/11, military personnel were used to police the U.S. posts and stayed on while the borders had closed for the virus. The countries had just begun to reopen but for those who manned the crossings, protocol changed daily and that made for testy exchanges.

At 7 a.m., on her call to the last crossing able to process their visas, she contacted the Deer Gate station at Champlain, New York. A woman answered.

"Officer Deo."

A dry spot on Annabel's throat stopped her as she tried to speak. She feared the woman would hang up.

"Hello," the woman said. Annabel heard Officer Deo bid a co-worker goodbye then return to the receiver: "Hellooo," she said playfully.

Annabel rushed to the sink, gulped water and spoke in halting whispers:

"Hello …. I'm sorry—I've told my story to a number of folks like yourself through the night." She wiped the water from her chin and took a deep breath.

"Okay," the woman said curiously. "Do you want to tell *me* your story?"

"Yes." Annabel continued with how she discovered the expired visas, why she believed that happened and the chaos their leaving would have on her little family. The officer was quiet for a long time.

"Hello …. Hello," Annabel said, fearing the guard had hung up. "Are you there?"

She heard the officer breathing then paper rustling and what sounded like a jar of pens falling over. The woman asked a lot of the same questions that the previous officers had: Citizenship? Employers? Where they'd crossed?

Annabel answered like a catechism student, quick and correct. When the questions were done, Officer Deo took a deep breath and said things to herself like *geeze, darnit, shoot!* Finally she spoke directly to Annabel.

"Here's what you're going to do."

Annabel grabbed a fresh page to list Officer Deo's instructions: Passports, certificates, HR letters.

"When you get here, ask for me." The officer could be heard opening a drawer and expelling another sigh. "I'm here till 7 p.m. Can you make it to me by then?"

"Yes." Annabel dared not say anything more for fear the help would be withdrawn. "We'll see you by 6 p.m."

"Call me if there's a hitch or you can't make it. Do you understand?"

"Mmhmm," Annabel mumbled. But said *yes* clearly when the other woman needed to hear it.

Annabel hung up and whispered thank you to the quiet kitchen. She rested her head in her arms on the table. Saliva returned to the back of her throat. She closed her eyes but feared she'd sleep given the chance. She jumped to her feet to rouse the others and gather the needed paperwork. Things could still go wrong at the border: Officer Deo could change her mind or be vetoed by a superior. What she'd learned in the many years of their crossings was that much depended on the mood or disposition of those policing the line between her countries.

Part III: The Message

Their boy slept for most of the trip. Annabel drove. Her husband navigated the routes along the northern journey. He studied the map on his lap—the interstates and their branches—and conveyed the likeliest spots for lunch or gas or bathroom stops.

Si loved maps, pointing to the mystery of the thin smaller roads or the wavering mark of rivers. He lauded the calculations of geography and distance: "It's high art! The lines for rivers and roads ... like Michaelangelo's hands." He'd hold the large, creased pages up and follow the weaving indicators on the map with his index finger pointing like the artist's rendering in the famous painting. After years, his proselytizing paid off. Annabel liked to squint at the charts he'd hung around the house to blur the random shapes of islands and coasts without their titles. She also felt a conflict with the hard line of borders which, surprisingly, were not as comforting as the swerving, jagged edge of natural shores.

But none of that was in the air today. Their bodies were tight and braced for what lay ahead. Rivers and forests and historical signs flew past. Crows flapped against the late fall winds, often flying higher to escape the current. She envied them their ability to rise above borders, then shuddered. When Si asked her why, Annabel didn't share the image that spooked her—the barrel of a gun on her temple and how, for just a second, she felt the cold steel at her hairline.

She shook her head again and wondered what haunted Si's quiet study of the fields and ponds in upstate New York. And so they travelled, riding in their solitudes until she turned off the 89 onto highway 2, which took them directly to the Deer Gate Crossing. The guard in the booth, when told what they needed, directed her to a bay in the carport attached to the main building. She slowed for three crows who moved, unhurried, from her path.

Si unhooked their sleeping boy from the back and followed Annabel inside. She turned to them just before she pulled on the glass doors:

"Maybe ... let me speak," she whispered and touched the arm that held their son's head steady.

Si nodded.

At the counter she asked for Officer Deo, and the fellow she asked assessed her seriously for a moment then disappeared into a hall that she hoped meant Deo was still on duty. It was 6:30 p.m. and though Deo was supposed to be here until 7 p.m., Annabel's expectations were low.

She could hear a woman's voice then, who—at first, had the cross tone of someone who wanted the subordinate officer to take care of it. Neither employee appeared for a moment and then the male officer emerged from the hallway and looked toward her.

"She's getting coffee," he said and rolled his eyes at another officer.

Annabel nodded and imagined a stark office kitchen somewhere among the hidden rooms. How casual they were, she thought. How routine for them, this day. Her boy was awake and made a whiny sound behind her. After a moment, she heard measured steps approaching. A dark woman rounded the corner from the dim hall to the bright outer office.

She sat her cup on the counter across from Annabel and didn't look at her. She held up her right hand to indicate she needed a moment. She tucked her shirt in a little neater and pushed a stray lock of grey coiled hair beneath her hat.

Annabel nodded. She felt relief that Officer Deo was Black.

"Okay," the officer said. "Let's see some passports, your husband's employment letter, and a birth certificate for Theo."

At that, her boy came running toward her and wiggled between her and the counter. After pulling the requested documents from the manila envelope, she lifted Theo to her hip. His head dropped against her shoulder and she edged the arm that held him onto the counter.

"Is this okay?" she asked the officer. Deo nodded that it was.

The other officers watched from their desks and every so often exchanged a look of disbelief with each other at what Deo used for criteria. The older fellow, seated beneath the painting of the president, shook his head several times when Deo would say, "That'll work." As the process continued, the heat in the building and the long day got to Theo; his eyes closed and his head fell heavier upon Annabel's shoulder.

As Annabel searched for the boy's Montreal birth certificate, her movements were restricted. She held the envelope firmly with the less free hand and pulled the contents from it with the other. When she didn't see the blue document, the hand that spread the papers on the counter began to shake. Deo shifted her stance a little—blocking those behind her from Annabel's view.

"You're the mother?" she whispered and pulled one of her cards from her breast pocket. "Forward it to me as soon as you get back."

Annabel nodded.

"Okay, I have to copy everything now," the officer spoke louder, gathered what she needed and turned toward the dark hall. Beeps from the copier, cupboard doors and the shuffling of papers could be heard. Deo was humming. This was probably her last task today. Annabel felt bad that the officer had forgotten her coffee on the counter, cooling. A dollop of cream had not fully dissolved into the brown liquid and had the effect of clouds in a night sky. The officer had also forgotten some keys she unhitched from her belt and Annabel admired the homemade keyring of small feathers attached to a braided ribbon. Theo's eyes opened for a moment, and she smiled at him for the first time that day. Annabel felt her body relax and managed to inhale a slow perfect breath from the unfriendly air. The other two uniforms had lost interest in her and focused on their own work—one of them on the phone:

"Is that *my* problem sir?" he said curtly before hanging up.

The fluorescent bulbs above the wide space blinked and buzzed a little, and—like the struggling light—an epiphany flickered and caught fire inside Annabel. The trials of the last hours finally gave some reward and not just in the renewal of visas. She looked around the vast room. Heat flushed from her core to her skin. The fear that had gripped her since morning broke, and giddiness flew like a bird around her stomach and chest. For a moment she worried she'd be sick. *My dream*, she thought—this is my dream. She laughed a little and cocked her head the way genius moves us when we finally see what we were meant to see all along.

Si walked toward her. He leaned on the counter beside her and turned his back to the two officers on the other side:

"Everything okay?" he whispered.

She nodded and smiled then motioned for him to take Theo. He took the boy and crossed the room to the orange chairs along the window. Annabel stayed where she stood but could not pull her eyes from them. She turned to keep them in her view and leaned back against the counter. Her thinking was logical and clear, like the steps of a ladder—each rung lifting her to a surer translation of the dream: For here was the father and son who did not belong easily to this country—her mother's country—whose birth there granted Annabel status. And though its borders were fortified with administrative steel, it was not impenetrable. But nor was the border between the living and the dead. Her mother and she had crossed that last night—it was the visas she was meant to find on waking—by the story told to her while sleeping. She thought about the term born-again and though she would be shy to use the phrase she imagined it was the right one for this: a new faith that life was not as random as she'd feared.

Outside, some crows teetered around the parking lot. The same three who'd walked ahead of her on arrival had now returned to the place where they must have scored food occasionally. For all the pitiless responses she'd received in the last hours, for all the hard-nosed posing that went on at these stations, someone fed the crows regularly enough to have the birds return.

She could hear Deo's steps approaching behind her.

"Silas and Theo Ames," Deo held the papers out for Si to take.

The father and son grabbed their jackets. Si pulled his on as he approached the counter and helped Theo find the sleeves on his.

At the car, Annabel suggested Si drive home. She said her spirit floated too drunkenly to be at the wheel. As they left the parking lot, the crows lifted off and flew high along the border between the countries swaying in the no-man's land on either side. Annabel watched until the distance transformed them to three floating specks and then to nothing at all. But they'd be back, no doubt, reappearing tomorrow as three crows in someone else's eye.

Four for a Boy
Watermark: 2014

That morning, as I stepped from the lawns of the old university into Roland Hall, l carried, for a few steps, the scent of magnolia and lilac into the anthropology lab. By the time I climbed the stairs to my office the outdoor fragrance had vanished from my clothes and hair but the lightness in my spirit held. The O'Neill play I'd seen the night before left some seed in me: a promise of immortality that shadowed me as closely as the April air had followed me in.

Yesterday, a friend had invited me to New London to see the performance in the parlour of the house for which it was written. The next morning, standing in the administrative hub of my daily routine, the O'Neills were with me still.

I cracked the dry sills of the old window behind my desk to clear the air. First in were the three notes of a sparrow followed by a breeze that shuffled the corners of the message slips on the spike by my phone. The cool air invoked O'Neill's mother's line about the fog—her dread of the sickly mist that moved in each evening below their home. In the audience the night before, I'd followed the gaze of the actress who'd said it while peering through the windows. All of us in the audience looked down the lawn to the water and saw, in real time, the ghostly cloud she spoke of moving toward us from the Thames. At that, a coolness pierced my core, as though the playwright's hand slipped beneath my ribs. I snuck a peek at the dark woollen suit on the man beside me but didn't look further for fear that I might have seen the mournful face of the author—the heavy brows, the dark eyes, the low voice saying, *I'm here alright.*

After the play, as I strapped a seatbelt across my torso in my friend's car, I saw the suit and the man wearing it leave the O'Neill's home. He stepped lightly along the sidewalk and disappeared into the late dusk. When he was almost out of sight he pulled a billed cap over his short grey hair and crossed the road toward Able's Tavern.

There were new tasks scribbled on the dry board above my desk. I recognized the department head's cursive in red and felt a fleeting sting at the gesture— she'd entered them above the list I'd left for myself the night before in blue. I knew then it was she who impaled those messages on my desk and imagined her hovering over the unopened mail that I hope she understood arrived after I'd left. I peeled the plastic top from my Sunstar coffee to begin my workday in earnest. Flipping through the booklet of messages, I found a childhood name on the last page: Anne Mallory. Could it be? The president of my high school class called? I saw for a moment her leather jumper and white boots, her straight hair hanging over her shoulder. I glanced at the mirror on the edge of my desk and wondered what thirty years looked like on Anne. She'd left a number but no urgent need to return the call. *Check your email* was the last line of the memo.

I scrolled my online mail until I found one from Anna Mallory-Stein:

Virginia:

Long time no talk. I am sorry to pass on sad news but thought you'd want to know. Mr. Caine passed away. They found him on the beach yesterday evening—our first good day of spring. Hope all else is well. Look me up if you're home.

Best, Anna

"Mr. Caine," I said his name aloud then rolled my chair around to face the window and the campus green below. I sat in the front seat of the third aisle in his high school English class. *Poor Mr. Caine*, I thought, remembering his corduroy jacket with the red vest beneath: the baggy knees of his trousers, the beige desert boots, his dry blond hair. The blue Corvette separated him from the other teachers in the parking lot as much as his barely contained vigour had at the assemblies. All that had made him seem younger than the other faculty—tentative in his dealings with others. Though as I thought of it now, he was not younger. The other teachers had marriages and mortgages and children, and most had grown up in St. Anne's. Mr. Caine had no family there, no wife or child. He lived in a little house left to him by an uncle. There was a rumour of a brother, but he never materialized, as far as I knew. Funny that a place with no family and few friends gave comfort enough for the man to relocate to where movies played only on weekends, two restaurants with identical menus closed at six, where one tavern and two churches were not particularly friendly to the newer folks that lived in their midst. He walked the beach a lot and reminded us in class that no one owned it, that it was everyone's heaven to the high water mark.

When he pointed that out, I knew he was right. We were, most of us, drawn to the shore. No one felt like a stranger at the edge of the Gulf. Foxes played along the surf, hares nibbled the dune grass, sandpipers with their twig legs motored along the wet sand just ahead of strolling tourists. The world of the village began and ended there. Even as a border, the sea seemed more a connector to the coast on the other side than a divide from it. We saw ourselves in the pastel seascapes the Art Nun hung between the shelves of the St. Anne's library. Though they were painted on a European coast, they had the same feel as our shore: the bleached light, the varying shades of beige and blue, the sprigs of beach grass along the dunes. The gold flecks that floated in the water and above the sand were ours alone, though— remnants from the mines that built the town.

Even now, when I return and walk that endless beach, the glitter on the waves and sand is like walking through a glow. What I long for when I tire of the city and my dull job here at the university is that radiance. Mr. Caine's house sat on the last hill above the beach. The lure for him had been happy memories from a childhood summer when he was sent to live with his mother's brother in the wake of a divorce—at least that's what the gossip explained about his appearance in our hamlet.

Poor Mr. Caine, I thought again, ashamed of the flirting I did with him throughout high school. Remembering how, when I knew he was watching, I'd move one leg a little farther from the other beneath my skirt or soften my eyes if he looked into mine for a moment. I don't think I said a congenial word to him throughout those years. Every encounter with him was a rejection of an unspoken sexual request, every exchange became a conflict of sorts in lieu of the thing I could not have. I couldn't douse the spark that stirred inside me when he walked into a room. My upper thighs tensed. And something short of nausea fluttered like a bird around my core until everything constricted and was at last reined in by my great effort to pretend that I didn't feel that way.

Below me, students had begun to spill from doors around the campus green after first class. A few raised their faces to the sun when they stepped from the shadowy awnings of the old buildings. Some lifted their hands, opening like flowers to the warm air. One girl ran across the lawn, flung her books to the side, and leapt onto a boy's back. Another settled beneath the Hay Library oak and leaned forward to warm her face. News of death is harder on such a day. I imagined Mr. Caine walking along one of the paths beneath me.

Smiling at the game of Frisbee in front of the Student Union. Shaking his head at the phones the students slipped from their back pockets. The canopy of leaves between me and the world below shifted in a breeze and I opened the window wider to hear it all: the moving branches, conversations—a buzzer, a car alarm, the line from a radio song: "I remember when rock was young."

I closed my eyes and entered that jumble of history we carry. The world only we know because of the steps in our wake.

One evening before graduation, exams were finished, decorating the gym was more an excuse for our class to hang on to those long evenings while we were still someone's child than a bid to make the ceremony look smart. I had volunteered to get the key from the office so we could close up on our own. On my way back, cutting through the courtyard that led to the open gym doors, I turned the corner into the hall and stopped short of crashing into Mr. Caine.

"Vi," he half whispered on seeing me.

"Mr. Caine," I responded and cleared my throat.

He set his briefcase down and hesitated. As I think of it now, he probably meant to check that I was alright, or wish me well—impart advice in these last days as my teacher. I scanned the halls and parking lot quickly.

Then, with a pounding in my chest and ears, as he straightened from the bend, I angled under him and brushed his lips with a kiss. He pulled back quickly, but his left hand instinctively reached for me and rested on the side of my neck, his fingers just behind my ear. He held the edge of my jaw and as if dared by the gods, pulled me to him. His lips closed over mine slowly, and then, soft as a cloud, he repeated it. Dizzy with the tenderness of the act, I leaned in until I felt his right hand cover my left. That platonic hold sobered me. His lips moved to my brow, then to my hair. He turned his head sideways and rested it on the top of mine. We leaned against each other until a voice from the gym began to wonder where the extension ladder had gone.

"Okay," he uttered, and inhaled unevenly. Mr. Caine, his forehead against mine, searched my face: mystified; frightened.

"I kissed *you*," I said to his back as he moved away.

He shook his head, turned it a little and stumbled over words.

"Don't," I said, meaning *don't say anything; don't ruin it*. He stopped at the open door to the parking lot. His case was still on the floor beside me. Mr. Caine took a few strides back. Before reaching for the case he glanced at me and held his right hand before him in a protective gesture. "Please," he said, to ward off any more angling on my part.

A slight anxiety had begun as my awareness of the work list on the dry board surfaced. I closed the window to the green below as my department head entered the Heaney Arch from the Science Quad. On the walkway ahead of her, four crows bobbed and half flew in front of her steps: "Four, for a boy," I said, and could not imagine the young, open face of Mr. Caine, vacant and white.

I slit open my mail and erased the first task from the list she'd left the night before. The heavy doors downstairs closed and slow footfalls ascended the steps to my floor. Rolling my chair away from the window and toward my desk, I sat again and closed the email screen. I imagined Mr. Caine face down on the stretch of shore we called The Cliffs though Anna hadn't indicated where on the beach he was found. He has passed through the door to the other side beneath the high water mark of St. Anne's beach. I touched my lips and thought of O'Neill and the man's elbow I brushed last night. There was something in the fellow's gait as he left, freewheeling and happy as he clipped along the street—as boyish as Mr. Caine before the kiss. There was nothing of O'Neill's ghost that shadowed him to the street though I did notice that he adjusted his hat in the window's reflection before entering the pub. "Still here," O'Neill would have said to himself before heading in for a drink. *Still here*, I thought, with my fingers on my lips as my boss filled the doorway with her presence.

Five for Silver
The Port: 1946

It is important to imagine the cliffs, the beaches and the woods as they were along that coast in the summer of 1946. Where an area called The Banks sat above the Gulf of St. Lawrence along the northwest shore of Cape Breton Island. Where a stretch of grassy bluffs hung above the broad cove of Port Ban, a harbour for the settlers who'd arrived a hundred years before this story began.

If you were facing land from the water—perhaps from the dory tethered to the small wharf on the port beach, you would see two houses, three hills apart. Closest to you would be Lily's home, a small red colonial above the beach in the narrow valley of Gold Brook.

The other house, Rose's, was north of that. A white peaked roof on a hilltop in the direction of town. You wouldn't see their laneways or the road connecting them as both were on the other side of their homes, but you would see the horse path closer to you, along the cliffs between the two places. It was steeper and more open to the elements but it shaved twenty minutes off the trip and could be done in half an hour.

Phone lines had not yet connected these homes to the world.

On September 5 of that year, the day opened like any fine summer morning: seagulls glided above the waves, swallows darted about the cliffs, pebbles rolled back and forth at the edge of the sea. Up from the beach you could hear the steady note of a sparrow above the other birds in the forest. A cow bawled from one of the farms. A dog barked.

Lily and Rose were the last of their people to stay on what remained of the original land grant. There were other relatives scattered around the county but none as attached to the place as Rose and her niece had become. Theirs were the only households in a three-mile radius.

Though Rose was Lily's aunt, they were only four years apart. They'd spent summers together as they grew and recalled those years like a golden road behind them. At the end of those seasons, when it was time to part, they'd hide in the barn or the woods, ignoring the first call for Lily to come to the waiting buggy for the trip to St. Anne's station and the train ride back to Boston. Lily would return to her mother's cramped quarters in the Waltham's home where she resumed her life as the tag-along child to the children of her mother's employers. For the most part, after lessons or meals, she'd play by herself in the window seat at the top of the house on Brattle Street until her mother, tired from serving all day, would climb the stairs and try to converse in a joyful way with her only child.

For Rose, those partings meant a return to her routine in the quiet house with her older parents; no hand to hold on the paths through the woods, no one to tuck in with or talk to in the big bed off the dark hallway. Her eldest sister, Lily's mother—nearly twenty years her senior—often felt more like an aunt to Rose. But Lily and she were to each other what they'd always imagined real sisters would be.

The arrangement at The Banks after the war was a happy result for both women. Lily's husband, Emmet, returned to St. Anne's after his service in the navy was complete. He and Lily fell in love in the summer of '41 and married that September. In that first year she travelled wherever his leave was granted. But much of their future was planned on the thin blue pages of naval stationery she received a minimum of three times a week.

"I'll be a good farmer. You'll see," he'd said in the last letter he wrote to Lily before discharge.

While Emmet seemed nice enough to Rose, it was their three-year-old, Findlay, that took hold of her heart. The boy, with his porcelain skin and silky hair, was like a breathing doll to her. Rose, for years, had prayed for a child of her own: she lit candles before mass, knelt at the altar afterward, bent her head and made bargains with God.

But when she fell in love with Findlay—for that's what she called it in her head—it was like a salve to all of that. Even her husband Hugh saw Findlay's effect on her and understood a little better her brooding when her monthly was due.

Within a year of Emmet's return, Lily was pregnant again. She'd told Rose in late spring as they were turning soil for a garden beside the red colonial. Rose didn't look at her immediately. She pulled a stringy root from the soil and shook the earth from it.

Lily's chest tightened. More than once she'd found Rose in bed, unable to face the days following a lost pregnancy. "I'll get you tea, darling," Lily would whisper when she'd find Rose upstairs in her big quiet house. Hugh would have already fled to the woods or the port—anywhere that freed him from the grief laden air of his home.

Rose, her thin face above the covers in the large bed, barely moved her lips to explain what had happened, again.

Findlay would crawl in beside her on such occasions. "Don't be sad," he'd say.

Like a switch flicked off, her pain was eased.

"I'll be fine, Findlay." Rose would turn to him. "I'm already better because of you." She'd pull her veiny hand from beneath the covers to tap his, or pat his head.

In the garden that day, Lily waited for Rose to respond. Both women stayed busy, neither looked at the other. Lily pressed the shovel into the earth with her left foot and flipped the sod over. She shook the usable soil from it before tossing the grassy scalp aside. In the quiet that followed, the gulls cried from the beach. A robin fluted in the woods.

"Here I thought I was getting plump," she forced a little laugh.

Rose heard the fear in her niece's voice. The gulls moved further away. Her neck and chest, her shoulders, everything tightened at the news that her niece would have another child while she remained without. She prayed to St. Teresa to plant a kind flower in her heart then stepped over the row she'd formed for the garden and reached for Lily's hand.

"That's good," she uttered. "It will happen for you Rose." Lily whispered without looking up. Rose squeezed her eyes shut. She felt Findlay's arms around their legs and looked down at him through a sad blur.

"Yes," she said.

When Rose pined too long for her own losses, she made things for Findlay. After her last period arrived in July, she made a sailor suit and two knitted vests. She saved her egg money for the white leather sandals she'd seen in the co-op. Rose made any excuse to take the path over to see him—hold his warm cheek against her own, comb her fingers through his fine hair. By mid-summer Lily tired easily, and Rose was happy to be of use. She went over several times a week.

On August 20 of that year, Rose set out to see them. This time she brought Findlay a cowboy hat she'd found in the attic and aired over the last few days.

"Is that my red monkey?" she called out when she heard him playing on the step. After the last turn by the big spruce, he came into view. He sat amid his toy trucks in the sandy mound beside the front door. He looked up for a moment, still vrooming, but returned to the mound as quickly. Rose sat on the top step and watched him. She put the hat on his head and tied the yarn she'd woven around the brim under his chin. So focused was he on his play that he didn't respond. She made much of the system he'd built of miniature roads:

"Is that a man there?" Rose pointed to a twig Findlay had been moving around the site. Findlay didn't look up. She asked about the cargo in the wooden truck. Findlay didn't answer. His head was bent forward, his face hidden beneath the hat. Emmet, who'd been chopping wood by the coal shed, yelled to him, "Answer Rose, Findlay," he said firmly, keeping an eye on them to ensure the boy acknowledged her.

Emmet waited. Findlay focused on a second twig and placed it in the passenger side of his truck. Emmet approached the step and knelt beside the four-year-old.

The boy looked up. His hat fell back and dangled from the red yarn Rose had looped loosely to the brim. She saw the grip he had on the boy's thin arm.

"Ple-e-ase," Rose whispered and bent forward to grab Emmet's hand. Emmet brushed her away.

"Da ...," the boy whined. He searched his father's face and squirmed to free his arm. Rose swung her legs toward the top step. The hem of her skirt ripped as she stepped on it and stood, then ran—arms flailing, through the screen door.

"He's hurting the boy," she cried as she tore through the rooms looking for Lily.

Lily struggled to rise from the sun porch cot where she'd been resting. She stepped into her slippers and ran past Rose to the front step. Emmet was back at the woodpile, white splinters of birch and split maple around his feet. The boy, still at his favourite place by the step, reached for his mother when he saw her. She eased herself down beside Findlay to let him crawl upon her lap. He closed his arms around her neck, pressed his face against her skin and released a muffled cry.

"When someone talks to him he needs to answer," Emmet yelled to them from the chopping block. He sunk the axe into the large stump and walked toward the beach, his arms waved dismissively as he disappeared down the hill toward the water.

The boy cried louder. Lily reached behind her for the step with her right hand and hoisted herself up carefully, her other hand still around the boy. Findlay pressed himself harder against her chest. She watched Emmet walk away.

Rose stayed in the doorway, both hands on her mouth. After a moment she walked toward the mother and child and embraced them both. She leaned her head against Lily's.

"Is he alright? Should I go?" Rose whispered to her niece.

Lily said nothing. She stroked the boy's head.

"We all love you, Findlay," Lily whispered to him several times.

"I'll go," said Rose. "I'm sorry I made trouble."

Lily grabbed Rose's hand and shook her head.

On the walk back Rose ran for a bit to relieve the tremble in her legs. She stopped at the open field above Slippery Rock where the ocean was loudest. She crossed her arms over her small chest and bawled for what had happened to the boy. Leaning against the trunk of a tall spruce, she looked to the sky. She prayed for Findlay to be strong in life. She begged too for her own sake—to ease her attachment to the boy a little.

On the morning of September 5, as Rose lay behind her husband, her right leg over his back—her mouth a little open and dry, cramps began in her pelvis. Twelve days late, she had gone to sleep with a plea on her lips that a seed took root. As she woke in the dark morning, something warm slipped from her. She pulled her leg slowly from where it rested over Hugh's hip and slipped quietly from the bedcovers. Tiptoeing on the cool floorboards, she grabbed Hugh's bathrobe from the foot of the bed with one hand, pressed the other between her legs and dashed toward the commode in the alcove by the hall window. She lifted the wooden top and sat. The blood was heavy. Sometimes a small mass slipped from her. Rose looked out at the black air. Small dots of light were moving into the darkness. Within a moment, the sheep in the backfield and the two cows were visible. She sat for a long time and watched the day begin. Morning moved over their farm with a pale brush. Dark clumps that hid the edges of the roses along the fence, lightened. The shadows obscuring the forest edge were removed—individual branches of spruce at the end of the pasture were clear now. The morning birds stirred. She was not pregnant anymore. Her hope was gone but she was calm.

Rose poured fresh water from the pitcher to the bowl and soaped up a cloth to clean herself. She secured a pad to a belt. She poured the soapy water into the chamber pot, slid the bowl out and descended the stairs carefully. Leaving it at the front door, she entered the kitchen to check herself in the cupboard mirror. She pinned her hair up, sliding a few wiry greys into the darker folds. She moved back across the room, opened the door and walked the waste slowly to the outhouse.

Spears of sunlight broke into the yard. A thrush called out. She rinsed the pot with pump water and left it in a path of sun to dry. Rose walked to the front step to warm her bare feet on the stones and lifted her face to the heavens.

"Okay then," she whispered, as if to answer the thrush. "Okay."

Before going back in she walked toward the wood-pile. Rocking the axe back and forth she freed it from the stump where it had been left. Holding it above her head, she swiped down and sliced the block in two. Birds flushed from the tree beside her. Crows and sparrows and starlings flew over the house toward the port; cawing and twittering; flapping their wings. She chipped some kindling off the larger pieces and stacked what she'd cut in the crook of her arm.

Inside, Rose dropped the big bits into the scuttle and lit the smaller pieces in the stove. The crackling fire overrode the winged commotion she'd started outside. Through the back window, facing the shore, she saw the last of the birds fly toward the sea. They're off to wake Lily, she thought, and envied them how quickly they could fly a few miles.

After breakfast Rose grabbed the lightest shift she could find among her summer dresses in the hall closet. She stepped into Hugh's boots and laboured to the crest of the hill behind the house where the birds had disappeared an hour before. She wanted a glimpse of Lily's place. Everything between them had fully bloomed since she'd stood here in July. The spruce, alone, had grown a foot. She could see the ocean and Hugh's boat puttering just beyond the port.

Tippy made his way to her and nudged her bare calf with his wet nose.

"Ahh." She knelt beside him and pressed her cheek to the top of his head. He pushed his snout up, his course tongue licked her temple. Rose jumped to her feet and wiped the slime away with the back of her hand.

"Come on Tippy, Tippy-Tim, Tippy-Tim." She ran back to the yard, kicked the boots off at the step and entered the house with the dog at her heels.

Lily was awake by the time the birds arrived on her roof. She saw the smaller ones dive past the bedroom window to the shrubs and trees around the sills of her home. She adjusted her head on the pillow.

"How are you?" Emmet stirred behind her.

"Fat and tired," she said without turning toward him.

He slid his hands beneath her nightdress and rubbed her back and sides. She closed her eyes and dozed again. His calloused palms on her skin made a chafing sound that in her half sleep became the distant swish of someone cleaning bricks, scrubbing the edges of a hearth until the bucket spilled. Lily woke with a start then and scanned the familiar room. She grabbed Emmet's hand and held it beneath her ribs.

"She's here." They both stared vacantly upon the walls waiting for the small bump.

"Aha, she's down here," she pulled Emmet's hand just inside her hip, but there was no second kick and they never come when bidden.

"How can you be sure it's a girl?" Emmet turned to his side of the bed and swung his legs to the floor.

"I'm not." She rolled onto her back and watched him reach for his pants on the chair. The smallness of that reach created ripples across his shoulders and neck. The ropey muscle along the sides of his lower torso were like the pictures of David she'd seen in the Waltham's library.

"I'll tend to Findlay before I go," he said as he stepped toward the bedroom door. There was hardly a limp anymore when he walked, but always when he left their bed in the mornings, he favoured the bad leg a little. Each morning she pictured the cramped gunner's room on the warship where the hit occurred.

She could hear Findlay pushing cars over his quilt in the next room. There were bits of dialogue she could not make out between the two or three imagined characters he had driving them. She lay in bed a few minutes more as though she could tally a reserve for the rest of the day when she would be on her own with the boy. There were days when he'd run toward the sea—when she'd have to tear after him, lock his wrist in her grip and drag him back to their yard.

She missed the city—missed the convenience of it: milk and bread at the corner, bookstores and streetcars and toys for a dime. She couldn't argue with Emmet that the hills and shore and the small school weren't better than the noisy walk to Runkle Elementary in Brookline. She chose to move here too, having held onto the dream of returning for so long as a girl, that she'd never questioned it as a woman. She couldn't stay away from Rose any longer and now she couldn't take Findlay away. During the war she'd filled the boy's head with this place. They would sit at the window and watch the park across Buswell Street. She told him stories of The Banks—how it was like the park, only bigger. She told him about Rose and Hugh and how they'd spoil him with home-made toys.

"Again, again ...." The toddler would beg for more stories. She would indulge them both with her talk of summers there; stories that had no start or end, just pictures in her head she wanted him to have. They'd sit like that till dusk covered them. Then she'd stand, snap the light on in their tiny kitchen and set out two plates for supper.

"More," she could hear Findlay downstairs. Emmet always allowed the boy too much sugar with his porridge. Lily turned on her side and pushed herself up. She tied her robe in front so that a bow flapped from her large belly when she walked. Findlay laughed when she entered the kitchen.

"Look at Momma!" He held one hand over his mouth and pointed with the other.

"Are you laughing at me?" She pulled his hand away from his face and kissed his cheek.

"Ya," he said and carried a spoonful of porridge to his mouth. The boy's grip shook with the effort of getting the spoon to his lips. Much of it slipped onto the table. She wiped the sloppy path and thought how everything is a matter of practice: in two weeks, Findlay won't spill as much food; in time, Emmet will learn to live without a car and extra cash.

She and Findlay sat on the back step and watched Emmet walk their winding lane to the Banks Road. They, yelling additions to the list of items he was to return with, and he yelling yes to it all. They kept it up until he crossed the little brook where their voices faded and water on pebbles outdid any human voices near it.

When a response no longer came, Findlay began to play in his spot by the bottom step. Lily watched him. She grabbed a truck and made a road around one of the miniature hills, backed it up and took a load toward the boy's industry along another small ridge. A tingle crossed her abdomen.

"Yell to Da," she said. Findlay stood obediently and screamed into the sky where he felt his voice could fly over the trees.

"D-a-d-d-y!" he yelled and then waited. The tingle rippled to her lower right rib:

"Go up to the turn there and try ... don't go beyond it," she pointed to the spot ahead of them as though she could control him with her finger.

The boy, dressed only in shorts, ran barefoot on the sandy edges of the road. When he got to the turn, he stopped, pushed out his thin chest and screamed at the sky, "D-a-d-d-y!" His red curls swayed down his back. His body shook with the effort. Only the birds could be heard in the quiet that followed.

"Come back, Findlay." Lily rose slowly to her feet and watched the boy return. She held her belly as though she could keep everything in place with her hands.

"I can catch him, Mom. I'm a fast runner. I'm four now."

Lily reached for his hand: "But I want you to help me today ... okay?"

"Okay." Disappointed, he started up the steps but looked at the dusty mounds where toy trucks were parked. "Want to play?"

"Come in, Findlay." She grabbed his hand.

"Please, Mom, please play?" He pulled back, his voice breaking.

"Findlay!" Lily grabbed the screen door handle. "We'll go to Rose's and you can play with Tippy."

Findlay stopped and held back.

"I don't want to." But then he imagined the old dog chasing him; tumbling with him in the high grass—Tippy licking his ears. Findlay knew the squealing he'd be allowed and imagined Hugh saving him with a grand swoop.

"I'll dress myself, Mom," he said as he ran up the stairs.

Lily followed him up and grabbed a dress from behind their bedroom door. She moved slowly, listening to everything her body told her. She descended the stairs and pumped water into a clean jar. She buttered bread, wrapped it in a tea cloth and dropped it into her purse beside the water. She made a fuss over Findlay when he appeared in his new sandals and cowboy hat, then followed him out to the step.

"I can do it, I can do it." He sat on the steps to buckle his shoes. Lily moved to the line and grabbed a fresh T-shirt for him. The tingle came again. She gripped the medal at her neck and prayed under her breath then pushed the T-shirt over Findley's head and arms. The hat stayed on the step.

She decided on the port path. The spruce trees could help in their way, to lean against or pull upon. Findlay ran ahead and stopped for her at the steepest parts.

"Come on Mom, you can do it," he'd say, repeating what he'd been told by his father and Lily for any task he'd slowed at.

The pain had not recurred. But her legs were tired and her ankles had begun to swell. When they reached the clearing above the port, they sat. Lily pulled out the bread and butter and offered it to Findlay. His eyes widened.

"You're a bread eater, son," she said and pulled him close. He allowed her to cuddle him as he chewed and stared at the sea. A few boats dotted the blue miles between them and Margaree Island.

"Can you see Uncle's boat out there?" Lily laid back on the warm grass and watched the soft skin around Findlay's eyes crease in his effort to see. She held onto his ankle and closed her eyes. After reporting on the boats and birds and asking if he could fish with Hugh sometime, Findlay gave her his crust and pulled to free his leg.

"Is it time to go then?" She opened her eyes.

"No, mom, I want to check for swallows."

"Come on now, we'll go." Lily held his leg firmly and turned toward him. When she rose on her knees water gushed from her. Findlay stopped pulling. He looked at the water that soaked her dress and the wet grass beneath her.

"Momma," he cried out. His eyes had narrowed and his mouth opened wide as he bawled, "You peed … you peed Momma."

"No Findlay," she said as she sat back in the puddle. "That means the baby's coming, it's just water." She let go of Findlay and pushed herself up from the dampness.

"You mean today … she's coming today?" He wiped the tears from his face with the front of his shirt.

"Yes, Findlay, that's right."

"I won't look at the swallows, we'll go to Rose's." He made a show of helping her up, then pulled at her to go faster. She stopped him when the pain came and looked to his white sandals instead of screaming when the baby pushed against her ribs.

At times the pain swept everything aside and she reeled to the ground until the pictures behind her eyes brought her back; images of blood soaked grass and Findlay staggering about the cliffs, visions of her on all fours or Findlay floating in the surf as Hugh pulled his boat to shore. She'd scream then, her face against the warm ground, her hands pulling grass from the earth like hair.

"Stay close to me," she would say when the pain had passed and she could focus on moving forward. After one episode, when Lily had fallen hard, Findley lifted her purse from where she'd thrown it and slung it across his body like a schoolbag, then leaned against her back and wailed.

"Stay close," she repeated.

"I will, I will ...." He lay beside her and pushed his face close to hers.

"We'll walk between the pains." She patted him on the shoulder when they could stand.

The sea had turned dark. Lily looked instead to the hills before them. She grabbed the St. Teresa medal at her neck. Findlay ran ahead.

"We'll see Rose's from there, I think," she said. She called for him to wait.

"Ya." He stayed where he was and held his hand out for her to take. "And maybe Tippy will come," he added.

Two crows swooped quietly overhead and cawed from the ridge when they reached it. "Two crows, Momma."

"Yes, two crows—joy." Lily repeated the line from the rhyme.

Findlay ran on, unable to wait for her. He stopped to readjust the purse and resumed his run. Three more crows joined the others and all five settled on the crest of the rise.

"Wait for me," she said as she felt the tightening start again. She pulled the silver medal until the chain broke and reached for Findlay's pocket as he approached her.

"Ask Teresa to help you, Findlay." She pushed the amulet deep into his pocket.

"Who's Teresa?" Findlay felt the oval shape through his shorts.

"She's a helper .... She'll let you know what to do."

"Sure momma," he said absent-mindedly as he reached for the medal.

The port path had steep beginnings at Rose's end. All who took it knew you had to hold the cliff grass and lean into the hill as you stepped along that first ledge. Sometimes, though, the grass pulled out too easily and the descender skidded and skated until they found some place to stop, grass still in hand. This is how Rose fell that morning. Distracted in mid-step, she stumbled. Still holding a little sprig when she found her bearings. She was clutching the grass when she saw the two on the hill ahead of her. Findlay was lying upon his mother but she couldn't make out Lily's position. Rose ran. She began to yell. Waving her free hand in the air and holding the grass to her chest.

"Yoo-hoo," was all she could manage.

Findlay heard. He slid from where he lay on his mother's back to the ground and squinted in the direction of the sound. Rose's dress and apron were flying around her and sometimes tangling between her legs. He moved toward her, then back to his mother, then toward her again.

"You're alright … you're alright," Rose repeated as she neared them. Lily, crouched on the ground, reached for Findlay but grabbed at the grass beside him.

"Oh, Lily." Rose helped her niece turn over and wiped her face with her apron. "You'll be alright."

Lily opened her eyes.

Rose scanned Lily's body quickly, patting her belly before lifting her dress "There's no blood, we're okay."

Findlay jumped on Rose's back. "We're okay," he squealed and laughed and clung to his mother's aunt.

She turned and pulled the boy to her, knelt before him and held him by the shoulders. "We'll wait until your mother's pain passes and then we'll get on either side of her, help her stand and pull her along, okay?"

"Okay," Findlay said and ran to the other side of his mother. Lily rolled onto her side and then raised herself on her knees.

"You came," Lily said, "you came."

"You've been in my head all morning." Rose reached behind Lily's back. Findlay grabbed her hand. They formed a brace behind his mother and hoisted Lily to her feet. Rose looked across the pregnant woman's belly to the boy:

"It was you, you little mug; the breeze brought your voice to me as I was starting up the path."

"Here it comes," Lily's body tightened. Rose and Findlay eased her down and settled beside her.

"Just go ahead and scream," Rose said.

And Findlay repeated it, "Just scream Mom."

Lily let herself go then; she leaned forward, turned her face to the ocean and howled. In the midst of the screams, Rose stood and ran toward the next hill. She cocked her head to hear the road.

"It's a car," she yelled back several times until Lily's screams subsided. She yelled again, "It's a car! I'm going to run for it."

Rose moved quickly out of sight. Findlay stood and followed a few steps then came back to sit beside his mother. He wailed. "Why did Rose go? We need her, Momma."

Lily reached up for the boy and pulled him down to her.

"She ran for a car ... we'll be alright," she brushed her hand across his face and wiped the tears aside. "Look at the clouds, Findlay .... What do you see?"

"I don't know," the boy was slow to partake. He wiped the wetness she'd missed along his temple.

"That guy has a beard," he pointed to the fluffy white cumulus above them. The cloud quilted across one fourth of the sky, blue and grey at the folds and at times, blocked the sun. It moved quickly above them. Findlay's eyes grew heavy. The old dog made his way toward them and flopped on the grass beside Lily. She felt the tightness begin again and reached for the boy. She looked to the sky before the pain arrived and saw five crows making their way toward the road. They fought in midair, twinning up and chasing the leader, diving for the medal that dangled from its beak. Before she closed her eyes she saw Teresa slip from the lead crow's mouth, the silver flickered in the sun, slicing the air when upright and slowing to a glide when flat—almost floating, as she sank and feathered toward the earth.

Six for Gold
Time: 1956

The calico had followed her to the crossroads. She'd never trailed anyone along the road before and Lily, though she'd looked forward to this walk all day, felt it added to the strangeness of her little journey. That the kids were not running around her with their piping voices and hot hands grabbing felt foreign enough. But this, this from the oldest barn cat? No, Lily didn't like the presage here. *What does the calico know?*

She walked back to the cat and eased down on her haunches. Lily stroked her back and spoke to her like a peer. "We can't both leave this evening." She bent her head and continued in a higher pitch, whispering, "And your young are still blind, bare babies mewling in the loft."

The calico gazed at the gravel hill beside them.

"Go on, now." Lily rose and tapped her foot in front of the cat then turned in the direction of town. After a few steps she looked back. The calico hadn't moved.

"Go on," Lily said again and this time waved her hands and stomped a little louder. The cat turned toward home—her sagging belly swayed and skimmed the loose gravel on the dirt road.

The dress Lily wore, she hadn't worn in years. It pulled in funny places now—twisted a little at her middle and stayed there until she straightened it with her hands. Still, the fabric felt cool and slick against the rolls at her waist. She felt stylish with her white sandals and nylon shift. If the kids were with her, she'd be worried and flustered, grabbing their hands and fretting about cars—though not one had passed her on the way to town.

St. Anne's, as she crested the hill, was flooded with evening light. It was mid-summer and she considered this time of the day the golden hour, everything brushed with a blond-to-brilliant glow.

The main street was quiet. Only the Greek was about, sweeping the dust from the steps of his small store. Lily watched him from across the street and held her left hand over her eyes to temper the sun from that direction. In his long white apron and rolled sleeves, he picked and brushed the small debris from the cement stairs and then began on the parking lot. Harry, he said to call him whenever she and the kids passed on that side of the road. He was a big man, wide. His walk was not easy but you could tell he'd grown accustomed to accommodating whatever affected his step; he waddled just a little. Like most newcomers, he had a ready smile and he was kind to her kids, often signalling for them to wait while he retrieved a little gift of licorice or gum from his store.

Tonight, his business sign was down. It leaned against the building where his oldest girl was adding the words *and Jewellery Counter*, to the *Books, Toys and Magazines* already listed on it. The whole scene rippled a little in the evening heat as she watched. He waved to her and she waved back. The ocean behind his business, smooth and still.

Lily resumed her walk through town. She felt the pocket of her dress to ensure the cash was still there: two dollars and fifty-three cents. The tightly rolled bills folded like an envelope around the coins. All of her money—always stored under the lip of a plate on the second shelf of her pantry, was now deep in the linty corner of her dress pocket.

Before she left the house, her oldest, Fin, came running from the TV room when he heard her scrape the coins from the counter. He watched her wrap them in the two single bills.

"You're really getting it?" Fin asked. He was just eleven but she saw glimpses of the man he would be—gentle, an ally.

He was excited to see her dressed up. "You look beautiful," he said, which brought Teresa running from the porch.

"Maum," she whispered, struck by her mother's makeup and dress. She ran behind her and reached for Lily's hair—usually in a bun but now loose, the bangs held back with a clip. She kept her eyes on her mother though Annabel, the next youngest who shadowed her everywhere, was at her side with her arms raised to be carried. Once on Teresa's hip, she reached for Lily. She moved her face close to Annabel and told her she had an errand in town. The toddler studied her face and rubbed some of her lipstick toward her chin.

"You little scamp," she said and leaned over the stove to see her reflection in the side of the kettle. Lily lifted the skirt of her dress and wiped the red from where it streaked below her mouth with a corner of the inside hem. She walked toward the door and turned toward them again.

"In twenty minutes, Rose will be here." She turned to Fin and said, "Can you clear the supper dishes?"

Fin nodded, still thrilled that his mother looked like someone else.

Lily turned to the other two. "Just take care of her, Tess." She nodded toward the toddler who was licking the lipstick off her finger. "You can't take your eyes off her."

Lily turned from her children and left without looking back—there'd be something to stop her if she did. She dashed across the yard and down the front lawn, brushing the soft tops of the peonies, pleased that the bluebells had not yet closed for the evening.

The calico must have seen her leave from her nest in the loft. She kept her litters in the upper corner close to the big doors that stayed open for the summer.

Where is everyone, Lily wondered as she glanced up the empty side streets and along beach road. She was disappointed that no one was about. She'd wanted someone to see her this way—the way she used to look—wearing all her possibilities on the outside. I suppose they're still clearing supper tables or getting ready for the races, she reasoned.

In front of MacPhee's Variety, she stopped to see the clock in the window and, if you could trust the sign—the store was open until 9:00. She had an hour. She thought she saw a waving hand from behind the counter but the glass was more mirror than window with the evening sun hitting it so she couldn't be sure. She waved back just in case.

Outside the Castle Tavern, a tall woman stepped from the doorway. Lily watched her, curious that a female was on her own there—especially one dressed as this one was. The woman lifted her arms against the brightness of the sun and staggered back a little. Holding her hands on either temple, she focused on the ground. "Oooh … Oh dear," she mumbled as she walked to the end of the top step and stood at the edge.

The obliviousness of the woman made it easy for Lily to gawk. The close-fitting dress was shiny and the skirt seemed to continually rise up so that she constantly tugged it down but one hand always shot back to the task of shielding her eyes. Her shoes were low heeled but had to be carefully placed on the wooden step so the heel would not wedge between the planks, and her greying hair was swept up in a French twist. How curious, thought Lily—this one didn't fit easily into St. Anne's culture. *Too fancy,* she could hear some say.

There was something familiar there—some history that Lily couldn't locate. She rarely heard gossip—living as she did outside the town—but maybe Emmet brought home some story that explained who she was and described her appearance in a way that made her familiar now.

Lily stepped quickly toward her to help her take the steps to the street. The woman was slim but older— you could tell by the fleshy edge beneath her chin. In her sleeveless dress the dimples in her upper arms and the bank of folding wrinkles above her elbow suggested years beyond Lily's. And as she drew closer,

Lily noticed the patchy translucent skin on her bare legs—*spider veins*, her mother called them.

"Can I help you down?" Lily walked toward the step to meet her.

The tall woman squinted toward her:

"Who's that?" she asked.

Lily touched the other woman's hand. "My name is Lily," she said. "Carrol is my last name, but I was a MacIntrye." She hoped the woman would make a connection for her.

"Of course you're a Mac," she said—a little snide, but she took Lily's hand and stepped carefully onto the sidewalk.

The door of the Castle opened and a rush of voices spilled onto the street. The bartender's head poked out and yelled to the woman, "I just called your husband. If you wait about ten minutes, he'll be along." The bartender looked at Lily then, "Would you wait with her, miss," he said and then mouthed to her some indistinct plea for Lily to do as he asked.

Lily nodded, a little worried about the closing hour.

The women moved away from the tavern entrance and stood in front of the store window next door. Levine's clothing had a family of mannequins on display dressed in the best they offered. It gave the two strangers a place to focus while they conversed and waited. The older woman seemed a little contrite about her last remark.

"You know I'm also a Mac," she said as she lowered her head and looked at Lily. Lily gazed back at the woman in the window's reflection.

"Ellen." The woman turned to her and held out her hand.

Lily was happy to hold onto the other woman for a moment—their touch might tweak some memory.

"You likely have a family as pretty as this one." Ellen seemed to sober a little as she nodded toward the window.

"Does anyone have that family?" Lily laughed a little as she spoke.

"I have three," Lily offered. "But they're with my aunt tonight."

"Ahh." Ellen nodded.

"What about you?" Lily asked.

"Look at those darling shoes." Ellen tapped on the window at the baby shoes dangling from the mother mannequin's hand: "For sale: baby shoes, never worn." Ellen whispered to herself and glanced sideways to see if she was heard.

Lily had just cupped her hands together against the glass to make out what Ellen was seeing when a car pulled up along the curb. A large man opened the driver's side and stepped out.

"Ellen?"

Lily looked toward him but Ellen didn't respond right away. She focused on the shoes in the window and tapped the pane. "It's the purest love, ya know," she said and looked sideways at the younger woman, "lasting and true."

The Castle door opened again. Amid all the voices, a line from the jukebox made its way to the sidewalk and Ellen sang along:

Together, at last, at twilight time.

A young man in blue work clothes, cap in hand, walked down the steps. The tavern door closed softly behind him and the quiet returned to the street.

"I love The Platters, don't you?" she said, still facing the window.

"Beautiful evening," the fellow greeted them as he pulled on his cap. He moved quickly between the women on one side and the man on the street before turning toward the track at the next corner.

"Now *he* walks with purpose," Ellen said as she watched him pass in the window's reflection.

Lily's chest tightened a little. She worried about the hour and asked the man beside the car for the time.

He pulled up his suit coat sleeve and turned his wrist from the sun.

"Eight fifteen," he said.

Lily gave a little squeal. "I'm afraid I have to run." She looked to Ellen and then to her husband.

"You go ahead." Ellen turned away from the window but did not look at Lily. She straightened her dress and tucked a few stray hairs behind her ear on each side.

"Bye, now. It was nice to meet you." Lily touched Ellen's arm before leaving and smiled at the man as she turned.

She could still catch Emmet at the grooming stables before the crowds arrived for the Trifecta.

Lily turned up Forest Street where bits of the sun fell in speckled light through the trees and buildings. She walked on the packed gravel, careful to avoid the soft shells of puddles with her white sandals. When she reached the highest point before the track, she stopped at the graveyard gate and looked for the peak of her grandma's stone. "Hi, Nanny," she whispered. Her grandmother used to let her ride, straddled on her lap, on the old swing outside her house. She could let go of the ropes and hold Nanny's waist, close her eyes and fly forward and back with the old woman pumping her thin legs beneath them.

Lily kept on to the arched entrance of Island Downs and stepped lightly upon the newly watered track. She wiped her feet on the centre green as she crossed toward the stables.

When she reached the feed window, she peeked in and saw Emmet brushing Fancy. Lily had only seen her a few times on the back of the truck and now took in how perfect she was—how sleek; a light brown mare with white socks and a dash of white in her bangs.

"Surprise," she said with a childlike smile.

"Lily!" Emmet turned and walked toward her. "What...."

"It's not that much of a surprise, is it?" She felt light and young—like the days when it was just she and he and an evening ahead for them.

"Is everything alright?" He was concerned.

"Yes, Rose is with the kids." They continued to stare at each other. Both of them a bit surprised at how the other looked without a child in their arms or around their legs.

"Oh ... good," he said and turned back to the horse.

Lily stepped toward a bale of hay at the edge of the stall gate and sat to clean her shoes.

"Kind of foolish wearing those here," he nodded at her footwear and passed her a clean rag. She tossed the hay she'd been using aside and filled the soft cloth with muck from her wide white heels.

"Well, I don't have anything else that goes with this dress," she said as she finished her shoes. She felt vain and shallow.

The announcer began to test the PA system,

"...and it's Last Chance pulling up on the outside ..." Lily looked toward the viewing tower and saw a few figures through the glass. The fellow at the mic was having fun, bouncing from one leg to the other as he made up names for bogus horses. He looked like the guy who'd passed her on the street outside the Castle. She recognized the cap he was waving above him like a lasso while another fellow was egging him on, hands raised in mock surprise.

"Out of nowhere comes a new filly, name's Light Legs ..."

Lily smiled up at them, longing to be a part of it.

"It's awful close to race time, Lily, are you here to bet?" Emmet looked over his shoulder at her and tapped his watch.

"Oh ya, Emmet, I'll bet that money we were going to use for the cruise," she shot back sarcastically. Her throat grew tight. She focused on her shoes and swallowed. How easy for him to be glib. She widened her eyes to hold the tears that threatened to slip and snuck her hand beneath her lower lids to wipe what was there.

Emmet chuckled. He began to braid the horse's mane. Lily stood and stepped carefully toward the mare's head. The horse looked at the boards before she turned her soft eyes on Lily.

"We should keep her in the barn at home." Lily smoothed out the hair along Fancy's chin and wondered where she'd wash her hands before leaving.

Emmet finished the braid and placed the under-blanket on the horse's back.

"I couldn't do this at home Lily, I'd have three kids underfoot wanting to help." He reached for the bridle and pushed the bit against Fancy's teeth. She resisted for a moment and then unlocked her jaw.

Lily stepped away from them.

"Well, Emmet," she said, "I'd like to buy a clock for the kitchen." She brushed a piece of straw from the skirt of her dress and lifted her feet, one at a time to inspect her shoes for manure or mud.

Emmet opened the stall and led Fancy to the buggy.

"I don't think we need another clock." His response was quick. Calm. He backed Fancy up between the buggy's shafts. "I'd better get movin' here Lily, I'll see you later."

For a moment she thought he was kidding. She watched him hitch the cart to the harness and continued to stare at the same spot on the Pari-mutuel wall after they'd walked away. He didn't return. She stood in the centre of the stall.

"Emmet," she whispered to the still air.

She continued a conversation in her head: *I have no time, no money, and now* ... Lily felt the weight of that and sat again on the hay bale. Then, like a door opened, she placed the woman she'd seen outside the Castle Tavern. Years ago, when Emmet returned from overseas, he'd waited with that couple on the platform at the train station. They'd been waiting for their own boy's return.

He didn't make it, was all Emmet said about it when they left them at the station. *Who,* she'd asked when they'd settled back in the dodge. Lily was focused on reversing the stick gear—it was tricky in the old car. Emmet probably answered but she wasn't hearing anything that day. The only words in her head were: *Emmet is home, Emmet is safe, Emmet's beside me.* But now, twelve years on, she crossed paths with that couple again. Lily was on her feet again in the middle of the stall, struck by this small mystery—solved. She remembered the stylish woman—her white gloves and her purse. *The McCormicks,* she said to herself. Emmet had been home a year when she'd read about them in Legion magazine. A half-page colour picture of them appeared with a rectangular black and white shot of their boy, Sammy, inserted in the text of the article.

Lily covered her own mouth now and bit her index finger when she remembered the baby shoes that Mrs. McCormick noticed.

There was comfort in the solitude and the distant noise of the jokers at the PA.

"She's leaving Chance in the dust ..."

Lily no longer wanted to be in the viewing tower. She cut across the track as close as she could get to the old exit. She wanted to be home and kept her head down until she was well along the path outside the track fence. She headed for an old cellar within the spruce grove where children hid for hooky. She sat and slipped her shoes off. She tried to calm her body. Tears would have helped but wouldn't come. She was sad for the McCormicks but their heartache was twelve years old. Her head was full of her children's faces and she longed to have them close—to embrace them like a litter and bury her face against their soft, warm skin. *The purest love*, Ellen had said.

In her head Lily began to rage against her husband—she yelled: "It's just a little thing to make life easier don't you see ... if I had a clock downstairs I would know at a glance when to start lunch, or your tea, or how long the bread's been in. I could work in the garden outside without the radio so loud it's like walking into hell to return to the house. I told you last week about the

clock ... that I saw it in MacPhee's ... that it was only four dollars."

She stood, took her shoes in one hand and covered her mouth with the other. She thought of Ellen. The track noises grew distant as she began to descend the hill to the crossroads. She was grateful that the path was soft on her bare feet and continued her silent railing *"I'm embarrassed when people are in, Emmet—everyone notices because everyone needs to know what time it is! God love Sadie, but when she was in last week I could hear her pity: "Dear Lily, a mother needs to know the time."*

She hadn't considered that he'd have an opinion on the clock. She thought he'd reach into his back pocket and pass her his wallet. She thought of him braiding the mare's mane, how gentle he was when he pushed the bit into her mouth. How Fancy relented after only a moment of resistance and how easily her request was dismissed.

Rose will wonder where the clock is, she thought, and the kids will be asking. She tried to calm down. She stood still and took a few deep breaths. Lily felt the tightness in her shoulders relax. She sat on the grass at the top of the hill and took in the view of the valley where she lived. She could see the house and knew the kids were probably in the window, watching to see her walk down the town hill. They would never think to

look here, the route they themselves used during the school year. They were excited for the clock. Anything new was thrilling for a second.

Lily closed her eyes and lifted her hands to cover her face. She saw the bluebells as she passed them in the front garden when she left earlier. How perfectly they hung from the arm of the tree—the stringy root that held them to the branch. She kept her lids closed and saw Ellen's bare arm and the Greek's shy wave. She remembered Fancy's eyes, and the calico following her—begging for something. She let go of her shoes and rubbed the sweat and tears from her palms upon the grass. She was surprised by the softness of the sod, she'd expected a little pricking from the spikey tops but the blades folded easily under her hand. They'd have to, she thought, otherwise they'd break.

A pack of crows sat on the ties of the railway tracks just below her. They picked between the coal bits, lifted their black heads to stare sideways, then fussed and pulled amid their folded wings. Lily counted six and took that to be a sign: *Gold*, she said to herself as she slipped her shoes back on. Her movement startled the crows and they flew up from the tight crowd they'd been on the ground as though flung by a hand toward the sky. She pulled her hair back in a tight bun and needled a twig through to hold it.

The slim end of the twig slipped under her loose wedding band and pulled it halfway off before it freed itself again. It had always been loose but lately she knew it would soon be lost—a calf she was feeding almost licked it off her finger the other day—and now this gentle reminder of its easy going. So different from her Nanny's thin band that dug into the old woman's finger like a string as she gripped the rope to hold them both on the swing.

"Doesn't that hurt Nanny?" Lily used to ask. She often touched the bulging flesh around it.

"I'm used to it dear, come on … swing, Lily … wheeee."

Lily pulled the ring off easily now and tucked it beside the grocery change in her pocket. She took the path back toward town and walked briskly to Main Street to catch the Greek's before it closed. The sign had been placed back above the door and she saw his daughter inside, wiping the jewellery counter. When Lily approached, the happy girl looked up, excited by her new business post.

"Can I help you, please?" She reached her hand toward Lily.

"I think so, dear." Lily took her hand, then placed the ring on the counter between them.

Seven for a Secret Never to be Told
Farewell My Brother: 2025

I had been waiting in Dr. Driscoll's office for 20 minutes, summoned by a letter that the doctor had written on behalf of my brother. There was no receptionist, only a sign on an empty desk in the waiting area that read,

> We apologize that no one is here to greet you.
> Have a seat and the doctor will attend
> momentarily. Make sure you press the
> button beside this note to alert the doctor that
> you are here.

Magazines were a thing of the past since the Medical Association banned them as spreaders of germs, and as I'd forgotten my phone at work, I took in the reproductions on the walls. A Degas dancer who looked like she was painted with a feather hung beside a number painting by Jasper Johns. Mediation, I wondered.

There was no one to question about the meeting. I had left several messages with the number on the letterhead in past days but no one responded. My daughter and husband knew where I was going and where to find me if they heard nothing from me by four o'clock.

My brother had stopped talking to me several times in our lives. The first was over a fight I tried to quell between him and our eldest sister. They'd quarrelled over their boys—one of hers and one of his. The young fellows had snuck out together after being grounded for the shenanigans of a previous night. When I felt the inevitable battle brewing in the kitchen of the family home, I grabbed my toddler and turned to leave.

"Where the fuck do you think you're going?" my sister said.

With my girl on my hip and my hand on the screen door, I turned to her over my shoulder—*let me go*, said the face I showed her. I nodded toward my daughter.

"We've got to work this out," she said flatly.

When I'd suggested that the respective parents decide what their boys could or couldn't do, both siblings turned on me. My brother and his wife resented my lack of support for them and did not speak to me for three years.

The next time we spoke it was I that called him. Our sister was dying. I had been with her for months and needed to return to the city in which I currently lived. Could he relieve me for a spell? He hadn't spoken to her since the incident and she was baffled as to why. She had alcoholic amnesia about most of her escapades in her drinking days and had decided he was simply an asshole. However, when I conveyed to her that he would be staying with her for a bit, I could see a sparkle that even her sickness couldn't subvert. There was a new energy in her voice and more patience for me in general. Siblings should talk to each other, she muttered as she grabbed back the grocery list she'd passed me to include his favourite foods.

She died a week after I left. He called me when she passed and spoke quietly into the phone. "Ahh, geez." He exhaled as though wondering whether he should he say it, then continued, "She was struggling for breath these last days, and hadn't opened her eyes since yesterday."

He'd been cracked open by her death, that was plain. The fog of grief had us in its spell while we arranged her burial. But afterwards, dismissed, I left the contact up to him.

So, eight years on, I am waiting in a doctor's office for some contact with my brother. Siblings should talk to each other—I heard my sister's voice from memory. I pressed the button again.

Finally I heard something stir in response: A faint cry? A door hinge? There was a knock before a tiny man stepped inside.

"We're glad you could attend with us today. Please follow me."

I stood when he entered and reached to shake his hand but he'd already left the room. I followed him down the wide hallway and was heartened by the quality of reproductions on the walls: Matisse and Wyeth, a circular sketch by Serra—something in this variety assured me of fair play, inclusiveness: safety.

The fellow I'd been trailing looked back and smiled before turning into another door. He was slight and guarded. I'd guessed he was gay and feared that meant he might side against me. The name on the door said Driscoll. I peeked inside, not concealing the cautiousness I felt. I expected anything: a back hand, a kind greeting, my brother and his wife looking at the floor, or the two of them looking at me, open-faced. The polarity of their presentation through the years was that varied. So, by the time I sat across from Dr. Driscoll, my anxiety was apparent. He stared at me for a long time, a vacant but pleasant look on his face—a vase waiting for flowers. With as much calm as I could muster, I asked him why I had been summoned.

"Can you not guess?" Driscoll said as he picked a thread from his vest.

"My brother?" I answered, annoyed by his indifference.

"Well, yes," he said more respectfully and with direct eye contact.

"Hum," I said faintly and turned away.

"Is it okay if I ask him in?" Driscoll was already rising from his chair.

"Can you guarantee my safety?" I asked, half-joking.

"Yes." The doctor, perturbed by my drama, frowned and left the room.

After a moment, I heard steps in the hall, my brother's familiar cough and the usual exchanges at a door when folks are being overly polite. I was ready to claw past them if my brother lunged toward me. He could be violent. His wife told me once that he grabbed her by the neck after a long day of following her through stores in search of the perfect lamp.

For a moment, when his shadow preceded him at the threshold of Driscoll's office, I was rudderless. Terrified: a mouse to a cat. His blue eyes darted toward me and away. He nodded. Driscoll closed the door behind him and sat beside his desk—the third point in our triangle.

"Okay," he said, a little nervous himself.

My brother perched on the settee, leaning forward with his hands clasped between his knees. He didn't look up. Another sad episode for us both, this. He was thinner. Grayer. I didn't shy away from staring and couldn't dispel the museum of scenes from our history that pushed themselves upon me. I saw the teenage boy who ran from our father on sock feet in the snow.

"Your brother wants to take care of some business," Dr. Driscoll began. As the doctor spoke, my brother's dark profile before the window reminded me of his silhouette in an older room. Beneath the natural light that pierced the cellar of our St. Anne's farmhouse on his last day of grade eight, he cranked the separator to divide the cream from the milk as I prattled on about my good report from primary.

"Oh, ya," he repeated after each reward I listed.

"Chocolate prize for health, stars for math grade and I got a twirlie thing for Art."

My eyes adjusted to the weak sun from the dusty window above that basement corner.

"Leave the light," he said when I felt for the switch along the wall. He wiped his face with the cuff of his free hand. Our mother stepped across the floor above us. The ever-present crows cawed from the trees around the house. Old Tabby emerged from the shadows and pushed against my leg. As though the cat had nudged the frenzy of my happiness into pause; the words our mother had thrown in my wake as I ran from the kitchen to show my brother my grades arrived, finally, in my psyche:

"Your brother didn't pass. Leave him for a bit."

I felt my brother bristle as though he saw the memory that played out behind my eyes. A familiar scent filled the room: it fluctuated between perspiration and soup. I would smell it in the kitchen when a scene was brewing.

Driscoll went on about Propranolol having run its course.

"Your brother's agreed to a trial procedure," he said as he gathered papers off the desk. Did that mean removing me I wondered, and what were the papers now on the doctor's lap? I tried to listen but my nerves got in the way. I heard bits of the doctor's diatribe and tried to focus. He'd talked about their discussions on whether to contact me or not. The words hippocampus and amygdala rolled back and forth over Driscoll's tongue like a hard candy. He added something about the minimal dangers involved but that the procedure is done regularly now without complications. I remembered reading about an operation for seizures wherein they discovered a process to modify memory. They'd been working on targeting traumatic episodes and deleting that history—at least the memory of them. The military dumped millions into the research and it had paid off.

"So," the doctor continued, "your brother's anxiety is rooted in childhood trauma that we haven't been able to manage." Dr. Driscoll paused and pulled his glasses from his shirt pocket. Too many scenes of a thin boy getting twisted on the floor beneath his father flipped through my mind's eye. The doctor held his glasses before his eyes while he read something on the top of the page.

"Okay," he folded the glasses back in his pocket.

"We would like you to sign an agreement. First, we ask that you tell no one," Driscoll glanced at my brother then continued, "not your husband, your children, your best friend, or your therapist."

My first reaction was to say no. The whole thing stunk. I mean, if you start tampering with our memories, what would become of historical fact? But remembering that my brother got the worst of it—that I learned off his back how to avoid beatings, how failures could gut you if you didn't step over them, and to never let my father define me as he did his son—I heard myself say, in a low and serious tone, "If that's what he wants."

There was no immediate response from the other two at that remark. Though for me, the fear that kept me tight as a drum till then began to ease when I said it. Momentarily, my brother leaned against the back of the couch and allowed his head to rest against the wall. I studied him for a moment. His eyes did not leave the ceiling. He took a deep breath, as though he were about to speak, but said nothing. He was relieved though.

Hope is the thing with feathers. The line came back to me like bait. A lightness began in my head and chest. Could this be a turnaround, I wondered. I looked at Driscoll. He was rattled. He bit the inside of his cheek. The features of my brother's face relaxed.

"Well," the doctor cleared his throat again and straightened the edges of the documents on his lap. He must have read the change in my demeanour or in the tiny smile I allowed myself.

"You must never talk to your brother again." His glasses were back on his nose and he watched me over the frames. "If you see him on the street, you can't approach him." Driscoll must have felt some pity because he added, "It's too chancy—it would impede the process. Your brother's future depends on this."

That I felt I'd swallowed a stone, I can't explain. Not even by chance did I see him in the city where we both lived now. He was a lineman and when they are not hanging from the sky to maintain our power, they are called upon when storms destroy transformers, or when accidents knock out poles in the dead of night. They are invisible fixers.

Only once, on the street about seven years ago, did I see my brother. I was leaving a bookstore in Robbie Square and saw him with his son. A cloud of pigeons filled the space between us and lifted off en masse when I stepped toward him. When the birds cleared, a quiet settled in, and a version of my brother when he was fourteen stood across from me. The boy knew me I think—his eyes lingered upon me until his father, having noticed, brought the boy's attention to the film at the nearby theatre: "We can catch X-Men at 2:30, son."

Driscoll was arranging paperwork on his desk again. I moved my eyes, blinking quickly to keep tears from pooling along the bottom lids. Crying always starts like a little fire inside—warm ashes gather in my chest, my throat contracts and dries; if we could howl, the thing would catch and burn out. But we don't.

I focused on the painting in the small office: Alex Colville's *Seven Crows*. I took my time viewing the beige field and the green forest. It was a small defiance of the pressure Driscol was applying. I imagined paddling the winding river beneath the birds—slow and calm—letting the natural flow move me toward the sea. In the field outside our parents' house, there was such a stream. Crooked Brook was a weaving tributary off a larger river that took its water slowly to the ocean—through cattails and rushes on one side, and on the other, a dark hill where the coal fell from the railway cars. I pictured my brother there for a moment and longed for him to come, to help me row to open water, to land together on another shore. But he was mired in the dark dust on the black hill, barefoot in the sharp coal. I knew, as sure as my heart was heavy, that I had no pull with him. I was a sister after all— younger, at that—and had no currency with which to bargain. He would root in the fossils rather than ride the moving tide with me.

Colville's clouds were full of rain but I stayed in the world of that painting for a while longer. I scouted a pull in along the banks. My eye moved over the two crows in the distance—hardly visible ahead of the rest. That would be my brother and I as we grew. Him in the lead racing to hide in the forest. Me in his wake—navigating the winds behind him as he flew away.

Seven crow a secret, I had whispered the rhyme he'd taught me that day when I followed him to the beach. He, trying to catch up to his friends, and I—struggling to keep up with him. Finally, in the clearing where an old hay road kept the spruce and fir at bay, where a smooth trunk of driftwood provided seating for us on our way to and from the shore, I found him in that cool, halfway point between the beach and home. He'd started singing the rhyme, and I asked him if he would teach me.

"Use your head to keep the beat." He nodded at the end of each line:

"One crow sorrow, two crow joy," and at the close of each phrase he dropped his head. I copied him and repeated what he'd said:

"Three crow a message, and four crow a boy." If I used my head, nodding to count the beat, the words were easier to remember.

"Close your eyes," he said, his mouth at my ear. He encouraged me to practise on my own, without his voice as a guide. Moving my shoulders to the rhythm of the rhyme, I remembered the words better and hoped for praise at how quickly I'd learned. A cloud crossed the sun and I felt the darkness through my closed lids. I called his name. He didn't respond. I jumped to my feet and glimpsed the stripes on his towel as it flew behind him on the last turn in the path ahead.

As quickly as it came, the cloud moved past. The sun warmed my shoulders and face. The ash leaves rattled. The flush of being left was still warm, and I prayed for protection from the coywolves and bears. I closed my eyes a little and gazed through the fuzzy slits to the forest and the clearing where I stood. Shafts of sunlight filtered through the trees. I was young enough to believe that God had arrived and adopted the sudden appearance of golden spears as my weapon against any harm.

I looked at my watch and asked Driscoll what he needed me to sign. He flipped through the stack of papers to the last page:

"I'll give you a chance to read that over," he said as he motioned to my brother to leave the room with him.

I signed the bottom of the last page and passed the papers back. "Here," I said before Driscoll left the room.

"You should read it," he said, annoyed again.

"Why?"

"Because, there are things you should know—legal things—repercussions for you if you … if you breach it."

I couldn't trust my voice not to shake or my hands to be steady. I looked at the painting again. I'd always thought the distant crow—the one the eye will almost miss—was a leader. But as I look at the crows following him—the ones close to the viewer, they are larger, menacing. They are *five crow silver* and *six crow gold* and I can almost hear the sway of their wide wings, the confidence of their flight. The front crow is running and scared and I will never know when he dies.

In The Shadow of Crows
Hart's Crossing: 1924

The child had been travelling for two days. On the second day she mostly slept, her head resting on the cold, damp window. In between her dozing, she watched the fields and farmhouses of the provinces pass by—her aunt's hand almost always on her back. She had been sick for so long that she was used to this weak and distant state that held her separate from the rest. She was happy for the touch of her mother's sister and slept easier with the weight of a warm hand on her back.

Often, in her half-sleep, she dreamt of a tower and heard, from there, her mother's worried cries about this trip. Something always slipped from the steeple in her dream—a crow or a feather, sometimes dust motes rode the temple light to the ground. And something would usually land on the seat beside her. A white horse came once. And then an angel who couldn't fit anything of himself into their coach seating—his boots banging on the legs of their foldable table.

"Don't be angry at your Mom," he'd said before he left the space, moving this way and that with a great racket. She woke fully then and gave sideways glances to her surroundings on the train: her tan bag and Teddy, and auntie helping a large woman with several children, squeeze past their seats in the narrow aisle. The child blinked to stay awake until her aunt settled into the seat beside her again.

"What a waste of time it is to be mad at me, Peanut," her mother had said at the station in Boston when the girl turned quickly from their last kiss. But she pushed the memory aside. She didn't want to think of her mother right now.

"Amherst Station," called the ticket man as he made his way through the middle aisle of their car.

They were approaching the Nova Scotia border when a second-wind stirred the spirits of the two travellers. All the grey hours of their trip seemed to brighten with the announcement of their provincial destination.

"Look," said her aunt, "aren't the horses pretty over there?"

The child raised her hand to the glass and sighed at the mare and colt. "They must be cold."

"No." Her aunt leaned over her shoulder to see the animals better. "They have the barn to step into if they need it."

Above them, the crows lolled about beneath the clouds. Her aunt said the birds were our best connection to heaven and their number gave us signs.

"See, two for joy." Aunt pointed to a branch as they passed it with two serious crows perched close to the thick trunk.

The child turned smiling at her aunt who was always making things better. She'd taught her how to "blow away" the pain in her ear when it reached its worst pitch.

"Like this," her aunt would whisper through the small hand the child pressed over her right ear. And Aunt would stand in front of her and fill her cheeks to bursting before she let the air out through tight pursed lips. The child had filled her most painful moments with this practice while her mother and aunt cooked up some new cure they'd read of or heard about: a poultice, a tea, always a prayer. So they read and fussed and cooked while the child looked on over ballooning cheeks.

But now, between their laps, they opened a copy of *A Child's Book of Verse* and began "The Tiger." The girl read aloud to her aunt and kept her place on the words with her finger, sometimes pressing the page so hard that the tip of it went white. And when "the stars threw down their spears," a rain began against the train window. She stood and watched the drops on the ponds and inlets, and on the flicking branches of the stubby spruce that grew too close to the track. They flew past the signs between the hamlets and sometimes saw a road. They passed a woman running from her door to her line, grabbing sheets and pins and yelling at someone they could not see. Dogs chased dogs, children walked with elders, horses pulled carts, and pastures and woods rushed by. Soon the pane was awash and slippery, and the outside speeding by was blurrier than before.

A tall man approached and held a pale hand in front of her aunt. "May I?" he asked as he pointed to the seat facing them. The older woman blushed a little but waved her hand to the seat and said that of course they didn't mind. The child watched him tuck a small bag onto the shelf above them. *What would a man need to pack that could fit in such a small bag*, she wondered.

"Hello there," he said to the child when he'd settled in his seat. She stared at him but did not respond, still thinking about the bag. He then smiled at her aunt and added, "She's a quiet little thing."

"Yes." The woman nodded. "She's never any trouble, that one." The aunt smiled proudly at her until the child turned and began looking out the window again. Her warm breath pushed clouds upon the pane and she felt a little dizzy, but the cool glass was nice against her forehead.

"You sound like you might be from away?" her aunt queried, shyly.

"The States, actually." He looked out the window on answering. The woman followed his gaze then, and asked nothing more.

The child heard the click of the aunt's knitting and sat beside her again. She loved to watch the mitt making, but also loved to look away for a moment in order to return to it and see how the colour grew and the garment formed. And she treasured the sound of the work. "Clickity tickidy, paws, clickity tickidy paws," she sang to herself and saw the words as she'd write them.

"They're beautiful," the man said. He studied the process keenly. "I suppose you're making them for your little girl." He smiled and nodded toward the child.

"Well, I sometimes just keep making them as there's always a child could use them." She didn't look up from her work. She nodded to the girl. "She's my niece, by the way."

"Oh," said the man to the latter remark, but didn't look away from the knitting. "How much would you charge for a pair like you're making?"

"Oh dear," laughed the woman. "I've never sold a pair, I usually just pass them over when they're done."

The child's eyes closed again.

"My boy would make a fuss over them," said the man.

And the girl imagined the fellow taking a tiny boy's hand and pushing the mitts on him, the boy teetering slightly. *This is what a father looks like* she thought.

The child began to drift off again as she leaned against her auntie's shoulder. As her lids closed against the warm cotton of the woman's dress, she saw the bag the man had stored above them and knew that it was full of tears.

"Drink up dear, you must keep drinking." Her aunt nudged her with the water bottle again. She noticed how her aunt's lips trembled sometimes, and formed words that were never spoken.

"... so that's where I'm headed." The man turned his hat slowly on his knee.

"Oh," is all auntie said. She had finished the mittens, wrapped them in a blue tissue and was tucking them into her knitting bag.

This time the child's sleeping took her back to her mother's quarters. To her very own corner where her bed was tucked beneath the dormer window; where Doll and Teddy sat at the tea table beside her and kept books open to stay busy until Momma finished serving. Her chest hurt from the wish to lie there again, to be hearing her mother's footsteps on the stairs—getting closer; feeling giddy as the latch on the door turned and her mother entered with a tray of goodies: leftovers from the Waltham's lunch. She thought the uniform her mother wore was perfect: the starched white apron and bib on the dark blue dress beneath. She could not wait to wear one herself. But her mother had swooped toward her at that.

"No, my darling, we will do better for you." She was folded like a kitten between her mother's shoulder and her cheek.

"Well, Sir, I hope things work out; I'm sorry for your loss." Auntie paused for a moment and then pulled on her coat and grabbed the girl's hat and gloves. She touched the child's cheek and forehead when she wrapped the scarf around her neck.

"She's warm?" he said, a little concerned. "May I take her for you? My father-in-law's to pick me up here as well."

The girl was lifted and took in the smoky scent that lived inside the woollen collar of the man's coat, and then the sharp perfume-like smell that came from the skin on his neck. There was franticness in being handled this close; she could feel little muscles clench at his clavicle and hear the unevenness of his breath. How different it was to be touched by a father.

They moved sideways through the aisles of the cars until she felt the coolness of the outdoors and the daylight seep beneath her lids. Her aunt followed behind and carried the man's bag. The child saw the blue tissue wrap in the side pocket of his case.

"Hart's Crossing." The trainman yelled several times as they stepped onto the platform, "Twenty-minute stop!"

A cloud of crows flew overhead then circled back, landing on the planks around the passengers. They hunted and pecked at whatever was thrown to them or forgotten by the travellers.

The coolness from the sea woke the child fully. The man stood her on the weathered wood beside the track. Her forehead scratched as it passed his chin. He tapped her lightly on the head with his free hand, then turned to bid her aunt good-bye. The girl held onto his hand a moment longer until he waved to another gentleman waiting in a buggy.

The air smelled like the skin of apples, and already her aunt was hugging an older man in a thick, blue coat. Beside him was another girl, a little bigger than she was, but still a child. Wisps of blond hair sprang from the green wool kerchief around her face. The girl walked toward her, then hugged and lifted her off the ground.

"You are so cute," said the girl. "I'm your Auntie Rose." She eased her back on the platform and asked how she was.

"Fine," said the child as she studied her new aunt's face. Rose had the same hazel eyes as her mother, and the same half-smile she'd seen a thousand times from her other aunt. Her new aunt touched her forehead as many had in the last few weeks.

"Poppa, she's burning up." Auntie turned to her father.

Poppa looked towards the child, squatted on his haunches in front of her and felt her forehead with his rough, cool hand.

"Well, hello there. I think your name is Lily," he said as he studied her face. "I'm your grandpa." He opened her scarf and folded her collar under it then re-tied the scarf. "Can I lift you to the wagon?"

Again, she was held by thicker arms than any she'd known before today. This tower wasn't as high but it was safe. He placed her on the back seat of the carriage. Her young aunt stepped in beside her and covered them both with a Bay rug.

"You'll be fine." Rose cuddled close to the smaller child.

"We're going to the convent on the way home," Rose said with her face close to Lily's.

Their buggy turned and moved onto a smaller roadway.

"This one was the most excited I've ever seen her," Poppa said to her aunt in the front seat about the young aunt in the back, and then added, "She's dyin' for the company of another young one at The Banks."

Her aunt in the front seat smiled back at them, then studied her niece in a more serious way. "She looks better already, Poppa."

"What's *The Banks*?" asked Lily who could not take her eyes from her new aunt.

"Why, that's home," Rose answered and pulled the small girl closer, kissed her forehead, then wiped the wetness from her niece's brow.

This ride was different from the train: rattley and bumpy with long quiet stretches. When they spoke, clouds spilled from their mouths and flew behind them into the wake of the buggy and the dark road. And when they reached the place called the Glen, there was still snow upon the fields; and that, with the white moon, made the whole country visible. The child felt as though they were riding through a postcard, and as she fell into a solid sleep against the shoulder of her young aunt, Lily knew she would write to her mother in the morning and sign it with circles and cross kisses.

Notes on Sources

Cover art, Alex Colville, "Seven Crows," Acrylic on Hardboard, Owens Art Gallery, Mount Allison University, Copyright A.C. Fine Art, 1980. Reproduced with permission.

Hughes, Ted. "Crow Communes," in Crow: *From the Life and Songs of the Crow*. London, UK: Faber and Faber, 1970.

Bukowski, Charles. "The Laughing Heart," in *Betting on the Muse: Poems and Stories*. Santa Rosa, USA: Black Sparrow Press, 1996.

Acknowledgements

I wish to thank the following individuals for their careful readings, their friendship and support throughout the writing of these stories: Chris Benjamin, Tracey Cassidy, Trena Christie-MacEachern, Andrea Currie, June Fliri, Denise Paige, Anne Levesque, Nancy Muenchinger, Frank MacDonald, Virginia MacIsaac, Deb Peterson, LJ McElroy, Eileen Rickard, Cassandra Tribe-Scott, and Joan Vincent. And to my editor and publishers: Blossom Thom and Robin Philpot—who were lovely to work with as they guided these stories to publication.

I would like to thank Arts Nova Scotia, The Alistair MacLeod Mentorship Program, and The Nova Scotia Writers, Federation for their generous support throughout this project.

An earlier version of "In the Shadow of Crows" appeared under the title"Hart's Crossing: 1924" in the anthology *Echoes of Elizabeth Bishop* published by Elizabeth Bishop Society of Nova Scotia. Designed and Printed by Gaspereau Press.

An earlier version of "One For Sorrow" appeared in the journal 'Magine: Unama'ki/Cape Breton's Literary Magazine. Publisher: James FW Thompson.

About the Author

Born in Nova Scotia, **M.V. Feehan** has lived, studied and worked in many cities and towns throughout Canada, the United States, and Ireland including Inverness, Halifax, Montreal, Edmonton, Vancouver Island, Comox Valley, Vancouver, Boston, Providence, and Dublin. She spent years as a reader and editor for the Vancouver literary journal *Room* and was a member and reader for the Providence Writers' Circle Annual Publication. Her work has appeared in Canadian, American, and European journals, and in the anthology *Echoes of Elizabeth Bishop*. In past years, she has received the Budge Wilson Award, The Hedy Zimra Scholarship, and the E. Bishop Centenarian Fiction Award. She completed her MPhil in Creative Writing at Trinity College Dublin in May 2021, and received the Individual Arts Grant from NSArts in 2022. This year she also received a place in the Alistair MacLeod Mentorship Program to complete her first collection of short stories, *In the Shadow of Crows*. Verna currently resides on Unama'ki/ Cape Breton Island with her husband and son.